PRESIDENTIAL
AFFAIR

CAUGHT
BY THE
CHIEF of STAFF

JENNIFER REBECCA

Caught by the Chief of Staff

Copyright © 2020 Jennifer Rebecca

Cover Design by
Alyssa Garcia
www.upliftingauthorservices.com

Editing by
Kayla Robichaux

For more information about Jennifer Rebecca & her books, visit:
www.jenniferrebeccaauthor.com

CAUGHT BY THE CHIEF OF STAFF

Secrets have a funny way of bubbling to the surface when you least expect them, and these are the deepest, darkest of all. I buried them in the past with my husband and any hope we had of a happily ever after.

But now he's back. Only, the sweet and funny sailor I married has been replaced with a political mercenary.

Can I trust him with the secrets of our shared past?

I guess there's only one way to find out.

For my baby daddy, Sean.

I love you with everything I am and then some.

It was only ever you.

THIS ADMINISTRATION IS OFF TO A ROCKY START

PROLOGUE

Gone

I clutch my phone in my hand so tightly I'm afraid the glass will shatter, and then where will I be? I just stopped the video. I'm going to be sick, but I can't now. I have to get to Rick. If anyone can fix this, it's him. I know we have a lot to atone for between us, but I know I can trust him with this.

My lungs burn with the air that isn't filling them as I race from the First Lady's offices to the main ones. I had come in to style Grace. She has an appearance tomorrow and two next week we needed to get everything squared away for. I love being her stylist, and life in D.C. totally agrees with my daughter Rachel and me.

Or so I thought. Now I'm regretting every decision that led me here.

"Stop, ma'am," one of the marines who guards the

offices says. "No one is allowed back here."

"I need to see Rick Donovan right away," I tell him as I flash my badge. My voice is thready, and my hands shake. "It's an emergency."

"Right this way, Ms. Donovan," Gus, one of Jake's Secret Service agents, says. "You can wait in his office. I'll tell him you're here."

"Can't I just go to him?" I ask. "It's important."

"No, ma'am. He's in a closed-door meeting," Gus explains.

"Oh okay," I reply. "Just… please hurry."

I pace Rick's office while I wait for him. If he doesn't show soon, I'm going to puke in his waste-paper basket. The offending video on my phone plays over and over in my brain on a loop. These things are time sensitive, right? And my baby. I can't bear for her to be away from me for one more minute.

"What the fuck could be so important that you've interrupted me during a closed-door meeting, Cara? Did you break a nail?" he seethes. I know he hates me; I hate me too. I did things he will never understand to protect him, to protect Rachel, and now it was all for nothing.

"She's go—" I whisper. The words get stuck in my throat and I can't get them out.

"Who's gone?" he asks, his body instantly alert.

"Our daughter," I explain. "Somebody took Rachel."

And poor Rick. He just found her, and now if something happens to her, it will gut him. I know he hates me, and I accept that he should, but Rick is a good man and an even better father than I could have dreamed he'd be. He is the way he is because of me and my actions, not because of him or who he is deep down.

"What do you mean somebody took Rachel?" Rick asks after a pause.

"She's gone, Rick," I answer in a panic. My belly is churning with acid and I know I'm going to be sick just saying the words. "Someone took her from the school."

I hold out my phone with the video queued up. Rick takes the little stack of glass and metal that hold our whole entire world in them. I watch as he hits play, his face is blank until the video starts and I watch the tightening of his jaw, his fingers whiten around my piece of shit phone, it's the only outward sign he gives that he's upset. Rick is a fortress and I'm that little piggy's straw house, one more gust and I'm toast.

"I think I know who did it," Rick says after a moment.

"You do?" I ask. "Well, go get her. We have to get her back."

"I'll get Rachel back if it's the last thing I do," he vows.

God, I hope it's not. He and Rachel need time to get to know each other after spending almost nine years apart. I don't want anything to happen to either of them. I love them both and always have.

"Please," I beg. I hope he knows I mean I need him to get our daughter back but also need him to come back in one piece as well.

"I don't know *exactly* who it is, but I think I know why."

"What? Why?" I question.

"Someone is trying to blackmail the president, and the only way to get to him is through me."

And then I promptly throw up in the wastebasket after all.

NEW CHIEF OF STAFF FEARED BY MANY

CHAPTER 1

Oh fuck

New York, New York

Six months earlier...

"You have got to be shitting me."

I never thought I would hear that voice again. A voice that had only ever spoken to me sweetly in the past is seething now, and I can't even blame him. There's too much history between us, too much water under the bridge. Even though he obviously hates me, my heart still pangs at the sight of his handsome face. *He looks good.* I hate myself for thinking that. I hate that I'm so drawn to him, that I can't seem to stay away even though I know it's better for both of us if I do so.

I picked my daughter Rachel up from school, and she bounced into the car with her normal high-energy motions. My sitter called me while I was sitting in the pickup line from hell to tell me that she was sick and couldn't make it tonight. Having once been a seventeen-year-old girl, I was pretty sure she had a serious case of teen hormones and the only thing that could cure her was her boyfriend's penis. I was young once. I could be cool; I could relate, so I told her that I hoped she felt better soon and planned to take Rachel with me to Grace's house to get ready. Rachel is a great kid, the best really. She's happy with books and a couple of games on her phone. I knew that I would be able to do what I needed to do for Grace with Rachel in the house. I had my doubts about what was really going on, and still do, but there was nothing I could do. It's not like I have a family I can rely on. Hell, I don't even have family outside of Rachel. I was an orphan before I married her father, and after that, I was a divorced single mother. It's not exactly an ideal life, and I would be lying if I said I wasn't lonely, but Rachel is one hundred percent worth it.

And I'm lucky tonight's client is Grace Sanders, a high-power attorney and my friend. I dress her for formal functions where there will be press or the upper crust of New York. Anything fancier than the normal. She has impeccable taste and really doesn't need me, but she uses my hair and makeup skills as well. And I make Grace look good. She's also really easygoing and loves my daughter, so she won't mind Rachel has to tag along.

"What are we doing tonight, Mom?"

"I have to work."

"Boooo," she complains.

"But it's Grace and you get to come with."

"Yay!"

"Hey, Auntie Grace," Rachel says when Grace opens the door. I'm not sure what I was expecting, maybe a butler or a live-in housekeeper answering the door now that she's living with the most popular U.S. Senator. He was gracing the tabloids with his bachelor antics before Grace won his heart. He's from an old money family, and I guess I just expected more.

"Hey, kid, what's up with you?" she asks Rachel, tossing her hair and making her laugh.

"Sorry," I say as I roll my big makeup tote in the house behind my daughter. "My sitter is sick. I think being sick means she's getting laid."

"Oh the good old days," Grace replies, and I can't help but laugh. She's not wrong. Back when I was married, I got laid all the time and took it for granted. Now, it's been so long that I'm not even sure all of my parts work anymore.

"Here," a handsome man in a suit says to me before lifting my heavy cart up as if it weighs nothing. He's handsome in a rough-around-the-edges way. I could totally be into that. Once upon a time and all. "Let me take that for you."

"Thanks."

"Wow. I think our stoic Gus might be smitten,"

Grace says, and I barely hold in a sigh. I wish he made my heart go pitter-patter, but it's been dead as long as my marriage. The only thing keeping me alive is Rachel. Before she was born, I was just going through the motions, doing anything I could to survive. Rachel and I are fighters, survivors; we'll always do what we have to in order to get through.

"Oh hush, you." I force a laugh and change the subject. "Now, show me what you're wearing, so I can work my magic."

"Right this way, boss." I let out a whistle when I get a load of how the other half lives. A girl could get used to this, but then again, I'm not the kind of girl who gets a fairy tale.

She leads me into her own private dressing room, and I take in the sweet pink ballgown with flowing skirt and bodice of gold beads. It's a great fucking dress.

"Holy hot Cinderella, Batman!" I whisper. "I fucking love it."

I stare at the dress and try to take in every little nuance. I picture it on Grace and roll through my mental catalogue of looks to go with it. She's one of my favorite clients, because she just lets me run with whatever I want to do, and she's always happy with how it looks in the end. Finally, the perfect look pops into my head.

"Okay," I say suddenly. "I've got it. Let's go set you in rollers."

She follows me back into the bathroom where I lay out all my supplies on the counter before rolling her hair up into large hot rollers. When I'm done with her, she'll look like a mix between a silver-screen star and Cinderella.

"All right, you know the drill," I order, and she rolls her eyes, making me laugh.

"You just like to see me in my undies," she replies.

"Don't you know it." I laugh. "And don't mess up my rollers either."

"I won't," she calls out from her closet.

She will. Grace always does. She's too hyper to be able to sit still and let me work my magic.

Grace hustles back into the bathroom and climbs into my chair. I dust her face with soft golds and shimmery pinks as she sits there in her underwear.

"I forgot my bowtie," the senator says as he tumbles into the bathroom to see Grace in her undies with her hair in rollers and me applying her makeup. "Holy fuck."

His expletive makes me laugh. He reminds me so much of the man I've worked so hard to put out of my mind for the last nine years—the man who every other doesn't quite measure up to—and not just because they're friends.

"Jake, this is Cara. Cara, this is Jake."

"Hi, Cara," he says, but he never takes his eyes off Grace, which makes me giggle even harder. *Ahh, young love.*

"Can I see you in the closet for a moment?"

"Absolutely not!" I practically shout, making him jump a little. "If she goes with you, you're going to fuck her, and then you'll ruin all my hard work. Fuck her later."

"You don't know that," he says nonchalantly, but I know bullshit when I hear it. "I could be careful."

"I don't think so, Senator Chancellor," I respond with a sweet smile.

"Jake," he corrects me.

"Jake," I repeat on a smile. "I've had a man look at me like that before. I know the look of a man who is at the end of his patience."

"Better get that bowtie and run," Grace says before she busts out laughing too. Grace and I always have fun when we hang out.

"Don't think there won't be retribution, Ms. Sanders," he tells her with a twinkle in his eyes.

"I would expect nothing less, Senator," Grace flirts.

And then he moves to his closet, and Grace and I wait quietly until he gets the accessory he needs and takes it to the spare room where he's dressing.

"Holy shit," I say, fanning myself. "Have fun tonight."

"You know I can't stand these things," she says softly.

"No. I meant after," I tell her with a look to the doorway where Jake just left. "That man clearly has plans for you."

"We'll see."

When I'm done with her makeup, I carefully unroll each of her curls and brushesbrush them this way and that before pinning one side back with a gold barrette. Grace rolls stockings up her legs, and then I hold her dress out for her to step into then zip her up.

"Here," I say, handing Grace the deep-pink lipstick I slicked on her lips, and I watch as she drops it into my beaded clutch. "Oh! Your shoes!"

"Right here, Cinderella," Jake says as he holds them out. She moves to reach for them, but instead, he drops to one knee and takes her foot in his hand and slips the heel on her before setting it back on the ground. He taps her other foot to let her know to lift it to his ministrations.

Jesus, that's hot.

I'm not gonna lie. I love Grace like a sister, but right now, I am all kinds of jealous.

"Thank you."

"And this," he says after he stands and pulls a long velvet box from his coat pocket. He snaps open the top, plucks a gorgeous diamond tennis bracelet from the silk pillow, and chucks the box onto the counter unceremoniously, making Grace smile and me laugh. He's such a man. Jake wraps the bauble around her wrist and then lets her go. "I saw it and thought of you."

"I don't know what to say," she tells him quietly, but still, I hear it.

"You don't have to say anything at all."

The two of them stare at each other for long moments, and I watch them openly. Romance, real romance, is so rare that you want to savor every piece of it, even if it's not yours to have. And then, the spell is broken by my ex-husband shouting the house down from the doorway.

I had a job styling my friend and powerful attorney to the fancy people of New York, Grace Sanders. Often, Grace would call me when she had a formal function and needed an extra hand making sure she looked absolutely perfect. For over a year now, I have been dressing Grace, and somewhere along the way, she became one of my closest friends—or as close as anyone can get to me. It's not that I don't trust her; it's that I have to protect my daughter. There is nothing I wouldn't do to keep Rachel safe and happy.

I haven't laid eyes on him in ten years, and even as his face is twisted in confused rage, he's still the most handsome man I've ever seen in my life.

"Is this some kind of a joke?" he roars as our eyes lock in the mirror.

"What?" Grace asks as I see she looks to Jake, who looks just as confused as she does. We never met when they were both in the service, so he shouldn't recognize me, but who knows how much those two have shared in the last decade. But it's when she looks at my face and sees it frozen in fear that the puzzle pieces all start to click into place. "Oh no."

Oh yes.

Unfortunately, Rachel chooses that moment to slide into the room on two wheels, totally unaware that one could cut the tension in the room with a knife. Oh fuck. I thought I could protect my baby girl from this for the rest of my life. Sure, she asks questions, but I've been able to evade them so far. I don't need to protect her from him but from the life he leads.

"Hey, Mom!" she calls out happily. She has big headphones over her ears that she asked for this past Christmas and probably can't hear anything. "Can I have a new game on my phone?"

I just stand there stunned. I don't know what to do. Do I pretend like nothing is wrong? Do I grab my daughter, who so obviously has her father's eyes, and run like hell? Do I hide her behind me? Throw my body on top of hers like we're awaiting a nuclear blast? I don't know what to do! What is the protocol here?

"Mom?" Rick parrots. I can see the wheels ticking behind his eyes. Oh fuck, this is not good. This is so not good.

"I can explain," I say, my voice quiet. "But not now."

"Mom?" Rachel asks suddenly, realizing the room is not a friendly one.

"It's okay, honey," I reply, hoping she doesn't make any sudden movements, but I also don't want to trigger a fear of her own father, a man she's never met before and shouldn't be afraid of.

"You have got to be shitting me," he bites out. "How could you? Is this some kind of a sick joke?"

"No," I reply adamantly. God, the last thing I want is for him to think I did all this on purpose. I had no idea when I met Grace that she would end up dating his best friend. But then again, why should he believe me? "No, you know me. I would never do that."

"I don't think I know you at all," Rick snaps before turning on his heels. "This is fucking bullshit."

And then he's gone.

"That was…." Jake trails off as we all think the same thing.

"My husband," I admit before turning to Grace. "I think we should be going. I'm so sorry, Grace."

"Don't worry," she tells me. "We'll talk later. It'll be okay."

"I don't know about that," I say before chewing on my thumbnail. It's a nervous habit I've never been able to break.

"Why don't you go to dinner and a movie on me?" Jake says. "I think you'll both feel better after some fun."

I feel my face go soft. God, he's just a nice guy. Even after knowing I fucked over his friend in the worst way, he wants to do something nice for me and my kid. "That's very kind of you, but I don't know."

"It's nothing," he says. "Joe will take you."

Jake made a decision, and Rachel and I pack up

the last of my kit before the cute secret service agent from before carries it back down the stairs for me with a sweet smile on his face.

"Well, shall we?" he prompts as he holds out his hand to Grace before leading her to their car. He's so attentive with her that it makes my heart ache. I'm so glad she has this, but at the same time, I'm a little sad I had it and it slipped through my fingers. But I got the best gift out of the whole thing. I got Rachel.

And just like that, Rachel and I are off to dinner and a movie in a senator's town car, all while my brain is whirring a mile a minute, wondering if he's going to ruin my life like I ruined his.

Or worse, what if my demons come home to roost once and for all?

A RUTHLESS POUNDING startles me awake.

Rachel must have asked a thousand times tonight what was wrong. I've never been one of those moms who unburdens themselves at the expense of their child, so I told her everything was fine and we should enjoy the movie. Which, of course, she chose the movie about the dog that is reincarnated over and over to find their person, and every time the dog died, I only cried harder. I'm sure it was an outlet for the fact that my world is imploding just when it seemed like everything was finally on the right path, compounded by the fact that our dog died a little over a month ago and we still weren't totally over it. But still, never trust a person who doesn't cry during a dog movie.

We splurged and bought all the snacks, drinks, and hot dogs to eat during the movie. At one point, I was sobbing so hard that I shook the popcorn bucket and it rained buttered globs over our laps. Rachel thought my show of uncontrolled emotion was hilarious, so she started laughing. So of course I had to throw a handful of popcorn at her, which only made my beautiful girl laugh that much harder. Her laughter is like music to my ears and always contagious, so I started laughing too. That is, until the dog died again, and I started crying all over.

Finally, the movie was blessedly over, and I could go home and mourn a fictional dog. It was late by the time we made it back to our small home in New Jersey. When I decided to come home, I knew it was going to be to Jersey. New York is wonderful, but New Jersey is where I spent my formative years. This is where I wanted to raise my daughter. I hustled Rachel off to get ready for bed and tucked her in not long after. My girl isn't one to dawdle. She's always set her mind on something and seen it through right away, no matter how big or small the task. She's a lot like her father in that regard.

Unfortunately, then I was left alone with my

thoughts. Would he take her away from me? Could he cost me my business? Could Rick send me to jail? Would he? He was so angry—and rightfully so. I can't help but wonder if he would feel the same way if he knew why. Would Rick still hate me? Or would he understand? But he can never know, because that would put us all at risk and void the sacrifices I made for all of us, to keep us safe—Rick included.

I must have paced the house for hours before finally deciding I couldn't solve the world's problems as they stood right now. The exhaustion of a full day topped with emotional upheaval finally sank in. I put on a pair of plaid pajama shorts and a tank top. I washed my face of all of my makeup and brushed my teeth before twisting my heavy mass of dark unruly curls on top of my head and slathering my hands and face with moisturizer. And then I curled into bed and finally, finally drifted off to sleep.

But not for long, because someone now pounds on my front door.

I grab the baseball bat I lean in the corner next to my bed and quietly creep down the hall. Everyone who knows me knows I have a young daughter, and they shouldn't be waking up my house at two in the morning. The neighborhood Rachel and I live in is a quiet one, but it's also not free from crime. This can only mean trouble has decided to darken my door.

I slide the lace curtain that covers the window in the front door back so I can peek at who is on the front step. Yep, I was right. Trouble is here and in the form of one angry ex-husband. I take a deep breath, flipping the locks on the door before pulling it open. Rick takes one look at me before he starts yelling.

"What the fuck are you doing?"

"I could ask the same of you," I reply, raising an eyebrow. "What are you doing here in the middle of the night?"

"I could have been anyone, and you answer the door like that," he says as he points to my attire.

"I looked out the window and saw it was you," I answer, raising my hand that's holding the old bat so he can see it. "Besides, I'm armed."

"Are you out of your mind?" he snaps as he grabs for the bat, effectively knocking it out of my hands. "This isn't going to protect you from someone like me."

He leans into me as he issues his threat. He's breathing hard, and so am I. We're so close our noses are almost touching.

"Should I be afraid of you?" I ask softly. I raise an arm to touch him almost against my will. It's as if the limb has a mind of its own, and it's on Rick, as I lay it softly on his hard chest.

"You should be," he says before he grabs me by the back of my neck and crushes his mouth to mine.

When we were together, Rick was a sweet and tender lover, and that man is clearly long gone. He used to touch me gently, reverently, and he always got me off, but it was nothing like this. He devours me without so much as a concern for anything else, his focus solely on me, and I would be lying if I said it didn't turn me on.

He backs me up against the front door and presses his hard body against mine, and it feels like I can't get close enough to him. I drive my fingers into his hair as he thrusts his tongue into my mouth and pull on the strands, making him growl.

Rick presses his palm flat against my stomach and skates it upward toward my breast. He molds my breast to his hand and squeezes it as he rocks his hips against mine. I want to wrap my legs around his waist and feel his hardness where I need it most, when he pinches my nipple between his thumb and index finger. I let out a whimper.

It's been far too long since I was with a man—this man—and I feel like I'm on a runaway train. I just hope I don't get caught under its wheels.

Rick drops his hand between my legs and dips a finger under the hem of my pajama shorts where he finds me wet and wanting. Oh how I want this man if just for one more time.

He pulls the front of my tank top down roughly to expose my breasts, and the material bunches up under them, lifting them up. He bites and licks his way down my neck, not stopping to soothe the sting as he goes, but it only ramps up how much I want him. Rick draws the hard tip of my breast into his mouth and sucks hard as his fingers pump in and out of my center. The combination of the slick slide of his fingers and the stinging nips at my breast has me gasping for breath.

Before I know it, Rick is shoving my sleep shorts down to the ground, and I'm stepping out of them. I hear the clank of his belt as he unbuckles it, and he unzips his slacks, freeing his hard length. His large hand is firm and strong on my thigh as he lifts it high on his waist.

And then he's there.

He's right there.

At the very center of me.

Slowly, ever so slowly, inch by inch, he enters me, he owns me, possesses me with a fierceness that before was just an echo of what this is now.

Rick lets out a groan as he fills me and drops his forehead to mine, closing his eyes. I force myself to keep my own eyes open and on his brutally handsome face. I know with aching clarity what it feels like to have everything one day, and it's all taken away from you the next.

When he finally opens his dark eyes, they sear me where I stand wrapped up in him. He dips his mouth to mine and licks across the seam of my lips. I whimper and open underneath him, letting him lick inside.

And then he begins to move.

Slowly, at first, he tips his hips back and slides almost all the way out of me before plunging back inside in one long, sure movement. His hand flexes on my thigh as he slides out and back in. I'm lost to him. I'm lost to the slick push and pull of our bodies, to the biting grip of his hand on my thigh where he holds me just a little too tightly. I'm lost to it all.

He holds me tighter as he pumps harder, faster. I can't catch my breath. There are no words spoken between us, and there don't need to be. Everything to be said between us right now is in the physical. Back in the day, Rick would worship my body with his, and I knew exactly how he felt without words.

His mouth hovers over mine—it's almost a kiss but not—as he moves faster and faster, his hips erratically meeting mine. And then he plunges in one more time, and I tip my head back as I fall over the edge. Rick thrusts once… twice… and then he growls as he finds his own release.

I hold him tight in my arms as he holds still, rooted deep inside me. I think this is it; maybe everything happened just the way it was supposed to. Maybe, after everything, Rick and I have finally found our way back to each other by chance and we're going to be okay. Maybe I can trust him with the truth once and for all.

"Why?" he asks softly. When I don't answer him right away, he hits the front door with the flat of his hand. "Why?"

"I can't tell you," I whisper.

"I just need one good reason why you would take everything from me," he says, and the words sounds tortured, like they've been ripped from his chest. He pulls out and lets go of me faster than I was prepared for, and I stumble to keep my feet underneath me.

"Rick," I plead as I take a step toward him. I can make him see reason; I have to make him understand.

"I loved you," he says quietly as he tucks himself in his pants and zips them up. "I would have given you everything."

"Rick, please."

"But not anymore," he growls before pointing to the stairs. "I'll see to it that she has everything, but you will never have anything from me ever again."

And then he skirted around me, slamming my front door behind him without a single backward glance. I flip the locks on the door before tumbling to the floor, where I hold my face in my hands and cry and cry. I cry for Rick and me, and I cry for Rachel and all the things that were taken from us all those years ago.

When the early-morning light starts to seep through the curtains, I pick myself up and slide my pajama shorts up my legs. I make my way up the stairs to my room and climb under the safety of the covers of my bed. But nothing feels like it will ever be safe again. I close my eyes, but I can't find sleep. I do find an acceptance in the way things are, and will always be, because of the path I've chosen.

And then I let every hope I ever had shatter into a million pieces and drift off into the wind.

PRESIDENT AND STAFF HIT THE GROUND RUNNING—BIG CHANGES COMING.

CHAPTER 2

Take it Off

Washington D.C.

Present Day

"May I have this dance?"

My breath seizes in my lungs at the sounds of that whiskey-smooth and all too familiar voice that leaves an afterburn in its wake just like the drink. All night, I've been standing in the corner like an old-fashioned wallflower. I don't belong here. I'm friends with the new First Lady, so I was invited, but I don't belong here with the political elite of our nation.

I watched as Rick worked the room, moving from one important person to another. People want to be in his good graces, and when he found someone he was happy with, his smile was blinding. I haven't been on the other end of that happy expression for almost a decade, and I probably won't be ever again, so when I heard him speak, I figured he was asking a woman who was standing near me as punishment. Ever since Rick crashed back into my life, he's been punishing me for leaving, for keeping his daughter from him, and—what seems to be my worst offense—not telling him why I did what I did.

He clears his throat. "Cara?"

God, I hope this isn't a new level in the game we're playing, where I ignore his attempts at public humiliation, and he calls attention to it so I can't avoid it. There's a lot of things I can take, obviously, or else I wouldn't have run away from the only man I've ever loved while I was carrying his baby. But I'm not sure I can take much more where Rick is concerned. Part of me thinks I should have elected to keep Rachel and me in Jersey instead of following my main client and my baby daddy to D.C., but Rachel wanted to get to know her dad, and who am I to deny her anything when I've made so many mistakes myself?

So I packed up our lives and followed him here. He made sure Rachel lives in a nice house and attends the best school. He's involved in her life like I always knew he would be if given the chance. Life would be perfect if he didn't hate my guts. Oh, he wants me, and he has me, because I'm a sucker still in love with a man I can never have, so I take him in whatever way I can when he's willing to give it to me. But every time he fucks me, he walks away hating me just a little bit more. And one day, these games will destroy me once and for all.

I squeeze my eyes closed and take a deep, steadying breath before I turn around. I'm expecting to find him in an embrace with a woman and he's just apologizing for it happening right next to me. Part of me knows I deserve no less. But part of me wants to demand so much more. So I'm surprised to see him looking absolutely dashing in a custom tux with his medals pinned to his chest and his hand outstretched toward me in offering.

Grace told me that Jake and Rick decided to wear their medals as a nod to their time in service. Rick had only been on the teams for a few years when we were together. He was young and carefree. Quick to smile, he always had a joke at the ready. Now he's older, more mature. He doesn't look like he laughs often— or at all—anymore, and he's feared by most people in Washington. It's hard to balance this angry man with the sweet sailor I knew and loved. But when he smiles at me like this and holds his hand out to me, inviting me to dance with him at a ball, I take it. I take his hand and jump.

Rick leads me out onto the dance floor and pulls me into his arms. Earlier, I watched Jake lead Grace down onto the dance floor for their celebratory dance, looking like a fairy princess. And she's got her fairy-tale ending too. The two of them are so in love, and they are going to change the world together. It's a magical thing to watch, and I love just being in their orbit. But it's also bittersweet, because my story isn't the kind with a happy ending—it's a nightmare.

"You look beautiful," he says as he twirls me around the floor, and I realize the song playing is "Just the Way You Are" by Bruno Mars. It's our song. It was playing on the radio the night we met, and we danced to it in the hotel room after we got married. It takes me back to a different time and place, when we were different people.

"CAN I BUY you a drink?"

I look over my shoulder, and the hottest guy I've ever seen is standing just behind me. He has hair that's almost black, and it's cropped shorter on the sides than the top. His eyes are like dark coffee. They heat me up while the corners around them crinkle in a smile.

"Cat got your tongue?" he asks me, knowing full well he's too beautiful for me to be able to speak. What is this good-looking god doing here with us mere mortals?

"Yeah," I answer in a breathy voice before I can enable my brain-to-mouth filter. "I mean no."

"Good to know." He laughs. "So what's it gonna be, beautiful girl? Can I buy you a drink?"

"Okay," I tell him. I shouldn't, but the way he's smiling at me makes me go stupid. It should be illegal for a man to look that good. I've never seen him here before, and I wonder where he's come from.

"What are you drinking?"

I feel my face heat in a blush, not wanting to admit I'm drinking the most embarrassing drink ever. Why is it in this moment that the most gorgeous man I have ever met is asking to buy me a drink, maybe engage in a little conversation, who knows, and I chose tonight to be cheeky and order something funny-sounding instead of my usual 7 and 7 with a ton of limes.

"Umm..." I start.

"Umm..." the good-looking guy repeats.

"A Skip and Go Naked." I cover my face with my hands, not wanting to look him in the eyes. "I swear I'm cooler than this normally.

"I'm more of a Drunken Sailor myself," he adds before turning to the bartender. "Another Skip and Go Naked for the lady, and me as well, when you get a chance."

"You don't have to drink it," I hurry to tell him. "I know it's silly."

"It's not silly if you like it," he says as he places his hand on top of mine where it rests on the bar top. "Do you like it?"

"Yeah," I answer honestly. "I do."

"Then maybe I'll like it too, or maybe I won't, but I

will learn something about you."

"You want to learn something about me?" I ask, feeling giddy and terrified all at the same time.

"I want to learn everything about you," he tells me. "But I'll start with your name."

"Cara. My name is Cara."

"I'm Rick. It's nice to meet you, Cara," he says as he holds out his hand to shake mine.

"It's nice to meet you too, Rick."

"Now tell me... what can I expect from a Skip and Go Naked?" he asks me, making me laugh.

"YOU LOOK BEAUTIFUL tonight."

"Just tonight?" I laugh.

"No, you're beautiful every night," he tells me. "Sometimes, I wish you weren't."

"I know."

He spins me out and then back into his arms before twirling me around the room. Rick is a beautiful dancer.

This is nothing like the way he would press his body into mine in the back of the bar. How hard he was, pressed against my belly or backside. It would burn me up from the inside out and I couldn't wait to get back to my apartment... *or his.*

Rick spins me out one more time before pulling me back in closer to him than before. His hand on the small of my back slides down just enough so that the tips of his fingers barely graze the top of my ass cheeks. I'm sure it all looks very respectable from the outside, but judging by the sizable bulge that's growing harder by the second against my belly, his thoughts are anything but respectable right now.

He holds me closer still as we move around the dance floor. One of his legs slips in between mine as we glide around the room and brushes against my inner thigh. And then he does it again and again. When he pivots us around, he runs his nose down the side of my ear, and I feel the puffs of his breath against the shell.

I feel his hard length press against my waist again just before the slide of his leg up my thigh, and I'm on fire. Rick is burning me up from the inside out, and there's no stopping it. I know he wouldn't try anything here in this room with all these important people and the press—not to mention the president of the United States, even if he is a friend. But I am so turned on right now I probably wouldn't stop him if he wanted to take me in the hallway. So when he leans in and whispers his temping words in my ear, I'm lost to him and his evil ways, and I can't even blame him.

"Want to get out of here?"

I don't even try to fight it. I just put my hand in his

and let him lead me astray, just like my own personal pied piper, all while knowing he will hate me in the morning. Luckily for me, I have a room in this hotel. So tomorrow when he's long gone and my heart is aching all over again, I'll be able to hunker down before I have to go home and pretend everything is all right in front of our daughter instead of doing a walk of shame.

I take a look around to make sure no one sees us leaving together, and so far, it seems like we're lucky. I watch Captain Black lead Jules off the dance floor and toward a dark corner and wonder what's going on there. Those two have been at each other's throat for days. I look back at Rick. I guess I can understand that more than I thought.

When I look back again, Grace is watching me with a sad look on her face. She knows better than anyone what our pattern is. Tomorrow will be nothing but tears, and then in a few weeks, lather, rinse, and repeat. Only she doesn't know the *why*. That little gem is left for me and me alone to carry.

When the elevator dings its arrival, Rick reaches to push a button, but I jump in and push the button for my floor faster. "I have a room here," I explain.

"All right," he says like he's granting me some big favor, a concession, when we both know that after a couple of orgasms, he's going to go back to hating my guts. Even though I can't blame him for his feelings, I still bristle against his words and tone.

When the doors open, I step out and start walking down the hallway to my room. I feel his heat behind me when I stop in front of my door, and he wraps his arm around my waist, pressing me back against his barely concealed hard length with the flat of his palm pressed low on my belly, just above the edge of my panties.

I snap open my clutch, pull my key card out, and slide it into the lock. When the light turns green, Rick reaches around me and pushes the door open, holding it for me to pass through. But when he closes it behind us and turns the lock, his sweet and happy demeanor changes to something darker.

"Take it off," he says when I turn back to look at him as he leans his back against the door.

"W-what?" I ask, startled. Usually, there's a little touching, a little reminiscing before we get down to the nitty gritty. Tonight feels… I don't know, rougher, darker. There's some unnamed emotion riding Rick hard.

"Your dress."

"Oh."

"Yeah, 'oh,'" he mimics me. His tone is teasing but also not necessarily kind either. "Now lose it."

I can see he's dangling by a very frayed rope, so I reach behind me for the zipper on the back of my black satin dress and slowly lower it. The fabric gapes, and I let the slim straps slide off my shoulders. I don't watch the dress but Rick as he tracks my gown's descent from my body to the floor.

I step out of the fabric and kick it to the side. There is something so vulnerable yet so incredibly hot about standing before a man as powerful as Rick when he's still fully dressed in his beautiful suit and I'm wearing nothing but a pair of black lace cheeky panties, my tall black heels, and some cheap fake jewelry. Grace offered to loan me some real jewelry, but that felt wrong somehow. Like I was pretending to be someone I'm not. So I politely declined my friend's generous offer and instead went as myself. It's not designer, it's not even real, but it's me, and that's as real as it gets.

"Lose the jewelry," he orders, and I pull the backing off of an earring made of long strands of dangling paste stones. I clip the backing back on once it's free from my ear and drop it to the dresser top before treating the second one to the same routine. "You shouldn't be wearing fake shit."

"I wear what I can afford," I reply as I slip the bracelets off my wrists and set them on the dresser with the earrings.

"Whose fault is that?" I think I hear him murmur, but when I look at him, his face is carefully blank, making me doubt I heard anything at all.

I roll my bottom lip in between my teeth and watch as Rick lets his coat slip down his arms before carefully draping it over the back of a chair. He pops one cufflink and then the other, flipping back his cuffs before pocketing the little gold links. Each of his movements is precise, exacting. His eyes never leave mine.

He reaches up toward his collar and pulls the tail of his bowtie. The knot springs loose, letting the ends fall open. His corded wrist flexes as he plucks each stud from the front of his shirt free, shoving them in his pants pocket with his cufflinks.

"Lie back," he commands me with his low voice, and I sit on the edge of the bed. I start to kick off my heels, but he stops me with a wave of his hand. "Leave them."

I use my hands for balance as I push back up the bed and lie against the pillows. Rick shrugs his dress shirt off and tosses it over the chair with his jacket before stalking toward the bed like a big cat. He pulls his wallet from his back pocket and plucks a strip of three condoms from the billfold, tossing them to the bed beside me before dropping his wallet to the floor. He unzips his pants and lets them fall to the floor. His cock stands long and hard, and he grips the base tight in his fist before crawling up the bed to sit on his heels at my feet.

Rick glides his hands down my calf, tickling me just a little as he raises my foot and slips the heel off before tossing it to the floor. He rolls the stocking down my leg before dropping it over the side of the bed and placing my foot carefully back down on the bed.

He slides his hand down my other leg, raising it so he can slide the shoe off my foot like a kinky Prince Charming with his Cinderella. He presses his mouth to the arch of my foot before reaching for the top of my stocking and rolling it down my leg. But this time, instead of tossing it aside, Rick twists it around his hands over and over. Finally, he looks up at my eyes, but what I see there, I'm not sure.

"Should I tie you up with these?" he asks. His voice is low and rough. "Should I bind you and punish you? Fuck knows you deserve it."

"If you'd like," I answer in a barely there whisper. The truth is I would do whatever Rick asks of me, just for another second with him, at his side, in his bed, whatever he will give me. And I'll take it gladly. But a secret part of me knows I'd love all of the dirty things he whispers to me when he's too far gone to sensor his words.

"Maybe another time," he says, studying me before tossing the silk over the edge of the bed. "But not tonight. Tonight, I need you to use your hands."

And then he grabs the waistband of my panties and pulls them down my legs. The cool air hits my damp pussy, and I let out a moan and arch back while trying to squeeze my thighs together, only Rick won't let me. With his strong hands on my inner thighs, he presses my legs open before dropping down between them.

There is no gentling me into his play tonight. The first swipe of his tongue is hard and brutal; the second forces my arousal even higher. And when he thrusts two fingers inside me, I twist the bedding in my fists and gasp as my climax rolls over me.

But Rick is far from done.

He sits back on his heels, rips open one of the condom packets, and rolls the latex down his rigid length. There are no flowery sentiments or pretty words, only silence as he leans forward and slowly fills me with one stroke while he leans his weight on my open thighs.

I deserve this. Every hate-filled look as he slowly drives his cock into my waiting body. He's burning me alive and flaying my heart open all at the same time, and still, it's less than I deserve. When his thumb skates over my clit, I know I'm done for. Another slow pass has me gasping.

Rick leans farther back, sitting on his heels, pulling me by my upper legs onto his cock. The movement impales me over and over again and pulls a whimper from deep in my chest.

"Touch yourself," he demands as he plunges into me again. "Show me how you touch yourself when you're all alone. Get yourself off on my cock with your hand."

I want to do just that. A shiver wracks up my spine at the thought of taking what I want, what I need from him and letting him watch me. I trail my hand over my belly and reach for my center where we're joined as he thrusts. I let my fingers wander farther down and feel the slip and slide of our bodies before drawing my hand back up to circle my fingers over my clit.

"Yes, that's it," he chants as his grip tightens on my thighs and he moves even faster still. "Fuck. Fuck. Fuck. Faster. That's it, faster."

"Yes," I pant as I move my fingers like I do at home when no one is watching. I feel my core clench around his hard length, and I arch my back as he drives me down on his cock again and again. I'm lost to the dance our bodies know so well.

"Feel how your pussy squeezes my cock," he growls as he pulls me over him harder, faster.

"Yes."

"Fuck," he bites out. "I can't hold back."

"Don't."

"Tell me you're close," he says as his movements become jerkier.

"Yes. I'm close."

"Thank Christ," he bites out as he thrusts deep one more time before planting himself deep inside me and shoving us both over the cliff.

I sprawl on the bed for who knows how long with my ass still draped over Rick's lap and his cock still deep inside me. In reality, it probably isn't long at all. My breath saws in and out of my lungs as I struggle to catch my breath. I wish I was paying better attention. Maybe if I hadn't let my walls down, he wouldn't have caught me off guard.

"Why?" he asks in the quiet of the dark hotel room. "Just tell me why you did it."

"I-I don't know what you're talking about." I do. I know exactly what he's asking, but it's too dangerous a game to be playing now. For years, I've been raising our daughter alone, all in the name of keeping them safe, but now that our lives have intersected again, I've had him but not. He gives me his body then takes it away again when I can't answer his questions.

"Just tell me why you left. Tell me why you left me and took my daughter with you," he pleads. It's the hurt in his eyes that cuts me to the quick, so I avert my own, unable to bare the devastation in his any longer. This round of our game is almost up, and once again, we'll both walk away losers.

"I can't," I whisper the truth, knowing he will hate me just a little more for refusing to tell him the reason why I left and should have stayed gone, all while hoping against all hope he would find us and we would get that happily ever after. But those endings are only for fairy tales. This is real life, and there are real-life monsters in it.

He pulls back, separating his body from mine. My instincts are to roll over and hide, but like always, I have to see this through to the end. I have to give Rick just enough to wound me even more, because it's what I deserve for what I've done. He can never know everything I did was for him and our daughter.

"Sometimes, I can't even look at you, and others, I just want to fuck the mouth that lies to me so prettily. So which is it going to be?"

"I can't tell you."

"That's just not fucking good enough anymore," he says as he prowls off the bed and steps into his pants, pulling them up his muscular thighs and zipping them. He tugs his shirt up his arms and steps into his shoes. He rolls his tie up and stuffs it in his pants pocket, and then he grabs his coat and slings it over his shoulder. When he makes it to the door of the room, he doesn't turn back, but he does say the words that tell me I've probably lost him once and for all. "You know, if you would have just told me, I probably could have forgiven you. But I can't keep doing this."

"I know," I whisper into the night, but he's already gone.

IS THERE A CONNECTION BETWEEN POTUS AND FLOTUS STAFF MEMBERS? TONGUES ARE WAGGING!

CHAPTER 3

Just let it go

Manhattan, New York

Six months earlier...

"Can we talk?"

I knew Rick was going to be meeting Senator Chancellor here, and I also know we need to find some kind of new normal, even footing sort of. If that's even possible after my world got flipped upside down last week when I saw him for the first time in almost a decade..

What I did not plan on was my long-lost baby daddy making an appearance.

In all the time I had known Grace, she despised Senator Jake Chancellor of New York. Never in my wildest dreams did I think she would hook up with the hot former Navy SEAL turned sexy politician. And then it happened so fast I didn't have time to prepare.

I knew Rick worked for the senator; I just figured I could avoid running into him. It was a naive plan, and it clearly had a snowball's chance in hell of working out. At all. But who would have thought a small time personal stylist with a very limited client list would ever run into the right hand man of America's most beloved politician? Certainly not me. In fact, Rick and I had lived in neighboring states for almost three years and had never once crossed paths. I don't know what I was thinking when I moved Rachel and I back to New Jersey. Maybe I thought I could be in touch with my heritage and introduce my daughter to a little of hers too. But all I managed was to complicate our lives ten-fold.

I had no idea Rick planned to meet the newly mint-ed couple at their home to ride with them. Or that he was about to be confronted with his long-lost ex-wife who had been living in the same city with the daughter he never knew he had. It was a lot to take in. I like to think I was prepared, but really, I was hiding.

And now, it's time to face the music. I can only hope I'll be able to live with the consequences after. But my daughter deserves to have her father in her life, and he should get to know her too. Maybe they'll be good for each other.

So I came to the senator's office first thing this morning after I dropped Rachel off at school. I just drove straight over here so I wouldn't be able to chick-en out by going home. I know from Grace that the senator drives her to work a little later in the morning, so there won't be a ton of people here to witness my shame.

My knees are weak, and my armpits are sweaty. I'm a regular Eminem song as I walk through the halls. I stop in front of his office door and take a deep breath before raising my fist and knocking.

"Come in," his terse words sound through the heavy door. I let my hand feel the cool metal before I turn the knob and poke my head in.

"Can we talk?" I ask his stunned face. Clearly, Rick didn't expect to see me here.

"Yeah," he says hesitantly as he stands from his desk and buttons his suit jacket. "Come on in."

I push the door the rest of the way open before closing it behind me. He gestures for me to sit in a club chair in front of his desk, and I walk through his spacious office and sit down. He has a corner office with huge windows that overlook some of the prettiest parts of the city. A huge wooden desk sits in the center of the room, a silent statement of the power and money he wields on a daily basis in the name of the senator. I can't help but look down at my worn jeans that fit a little snugger than they did a year ago and a pair of Converse sneakers. Maybe I should have put more thought into how I looked this morning before I came over here.

"So…" he starts as he leans his ass against the front of his desk with his arms folded over his chest. "You wanted to talk."

"Yes," I say as I reach into my huge tote bag of a purse. "I know the other day was a shock to you."

"You can say that again," he mumbles.

"And I know you don't understand—"

"I don't."

"But I brought you these," I say as I hand him a small pink photo album I made throughout the years for him and a small envelope. He opens the envelope and stares at the paper.

"My name is on her birth certificate?" he asks, clearly surprised.

"It always was," I say after I clear my throat.

"Why?"

"You're her father," I explain.

"No," he says, studying me, "I mean *why* did you run?"

"That's an official copy. I have one as well," I tell him, trying to change the subject. "That's your book as well. I've been putting it together for you over the years, just in case."

"Just in case of what?"

"In case we ever ran into you," I explain.

"Were you ever going to try to find me?" he asks quietly. I watch him carefully before deciding he deserves the truth, even if it ruins any hope I might have had for a copacetic situation.

"No."

"Why did you do it?"

"I don't want to talk about that," I say, batting the thought away. "It's in the past."

"It doesn't feel like the past."

"Just let it go," I quietly plead.

Rick watches me. He's deciding something but I don't know what. His face is so carefully blank. "All right," he says. "For now."

"Thank you." I breathe a small sigh of relief.

"I want to meet her," he says firmly after a moment.

"She wants to meet you too." That seems to take him off guard.

"She knows about me?"

"She does," I answer him honestly. I feel my heart soften just a bit toward him. Somewhere deep down is my sweet sailor. "I never kept you from her."

"Only her from me?" he asks, his voice hard again. "I want to be in her life."

"We want you to be in her life too." And it's the truth he can never know about. I had always wanted them to be together. I never wanted things to play out the way that they had, but I can't go back. I can't second guess the decisions I have made to protect my family now. I can only continue to put one foot in front of the other.

"I just don't understand why," he tries again, and I

have to put a stop to it before I start crying in the middle of his office and admit everything that ever happened.

"I won't ask you for money," I state, changing the subject again. "I only ask that you don't make life-altering decisions about her life without me."

"You mean like you did?"

I let out a frustrated breath. "I had my reasons."

"But you won't share them?" he asks again. Rick clearly missed his true calling as a hostage negotiator. Or a terrorist interrogator.

"No, I won't."

He looks away at something out one of the windows for a minute as he mulls over something in his mind. I'm sure it has to do with me and our daughter and what we're going to have to do to move forward from here. When he turns his head back to face me, I know he has made some decisions.

"I'd like to take you both out to dinner," he says, making me gasp. I'm surprised he would include me in his plans. "She doesn't know me yet, and I want you both to be sure she is safe with me."

"I appreciate that."

"How does she feel about pizza?" he asks, making me smile.

"She's eight and lives in Jersey," I tell him.

"So, in other words, she takes her pie as seriously as her mother always did." He smirks at me. It was a running joke between us that I was particular about my pizza.

"I still am," I say, smiling.

"I guess not everything changes," he replies, effectively wiping the smile from my face.

"No," I whisper.

"I'll pick you both up at five."

"Maybe we should meet you at the restaurant," I try, because the thought of having Rick in my space has me on edge.

"I said I'll pick you up at five," he states firmly, ending our conversation.

I'm being dismissed. The glimpse of my funny sailor is long gone.

"I'll tell Rachel when I pick her up from school," I say as I stand from the chair. "She'll be pleased."

And then I run away like the scared little rabbit I am.

"SERIOUS QUESTION," RICK begins after we sit down in a booth at a small, family-owned pizza place just a couple of blocks from my apartment. How Rick knew it was there, I will never know.

"What's that?" Rachel replies.

"Anchovies or no anchovies?" he asks, making her nose scrunch up.

"Ew, gross!"

"What?" he gasps, clutching his chest. "You mean to tell me you're not firmly in your mom's 'anchovies are life' camp?"

"No way!" She laughs at his joke, and it's the sweetest sound in the world. By the look on his face, Rick feels the same way.

"What kind of Jersey girl are you?"

"A bad one." She laughs. "I was born in Nevada."

"Nevada?" he prompts, even though I know he knows just about everything about her, since I delivered the baby book, her birth certificate, and a letter telling him all about our beautiful daughter this morning. He knows she loves soccer and hates the color pink. She's read an entire series on dragons in the last month and is allergic to penicillin. And that she's known about him and who he is her entire life. "So you deal blackjack?"

"No, silly. I'm a kid."

"You are? I thought you were thirty-five," he replies.

"No way!" She laughs again. "I'm eight."

"Well then, what do eight-year-olds do for fun?"

"I like video games and dragon books, and I play soccer."

"Soccer?" he practically shouts. "I love soccer! What position do you play?"

"Defender!"

"Sweet! I was a goalkeeper when I was in school."

"No way! I hate that position," she shouts, making Rick laugh.

"What can I get you tonight?" a young server in jeans and a T-shirt with the restaurant logo on the front asks as he steps up to the table.

"I think we need a medium—" Rick starts to say, but Rachel shakes her head. "A *large* pepperoni pizza, and a medium pepperoni and anchovies for the Jersey girl."

"Thank you," I mumble.

"And to drink?"

"Cokes all around?" Rick asks.

I smile when Rachel yells a "Woohoo!"

"So soccer, huh?" Rick prompts when the server walks away. "Mom didn't get you in a tutu and tap shoes?"

"Ugh," Rachel says, sounding very put out for an eight-year-old. "Don't remind me!"

"Oh come on!" I protest. "It wasn't that bad."

"It was terrible!" Rachel pouts. "I could have died."

"Don't be so dramatic. You were three."

"I was traumatized."

"Well I could send you to therapy or I can give you all my cash to play some video games. What will it be?" I ask her.

"Video games," she answers, holding out her little hand. "The SeaWolf will heal my soul."

"Oh it will, will it?"

"Yes." She nods with all the seriousness in the world.

"Here." I laugh as I hand her a couple bucks. "That should tide you over until the pizza is done."

"Thanks, Mama," she says sweetly before she places a kiss on my cheek. "I love you."

"I love you too, sunshine girl."

"She's something else," Rick says as he watches her hop away, and I can't help the pang I feel in my heart for all he's missed out on.

"She is."

The waiter drops off our drinks, and we both busy ourselves with unwrapping paper from straws and drinking more soda than is necessary just to avoid heavy conversation topics.

"I think we should buy two houses next to each other," he says after a moment. Unfortunately, that moment was right after I had taken a big sip of soda, and I choke on it.

"Absolutely not," I tell him. Even if I could afford a house—which I cannot—watching him date other women would gut me. I've been lucky so far, and it's selfish to say, but with him being out of our lives, I haven't had to watch him settle down with someone who was not me.

"Why not?" he asks. Oh, God, he's serious. I was hoping he was kidding.

"Well, for one, I can't afford a house," I answer honestly, even though my pride smarts at the spoken truth.

"That's an easy fix," he says. "I make plenty of money. I'll buy both."

"Not so fast," I say, holding up a hand to slow this train down before it crashes at heartbreak station. "I can't let you buy me a house."

"Sure you can," he says confidently. "I haven't paid child support in eight years. I owe you."

"You don't owe me anything," I tell him. "But still, no."

"Why not?"

I let out a frustrated breath before answering. "Sure, now it seems like a good idea. But what about when you're dating or when you bring a woman home? And when you settle down and start a family? Rachel won't understand why she's not part of that." I have to look away, because the thought of Rick with his own family is physically painful.

"Are you worried about your feelings or Rachel's?" he asks quietly, and I hate that he could always read me so well, and apparently, he still can.

"Rachel's, of course."

"Of course," Rick parrots. "How many lovers have you had since me?"

"None," I answer. "But maybe it's time I get back out there. I don't want your parade of women in front of my daughter."

"Our daughter," he corrects.

"I don't want your parade of women in front of our daughter." Or me. But mostly Rachel. I haven't dated at all, so she wouldn't understand. She's not a baby anymore, but she's also still a child.

"Do you know what they called me in the Navy?" he asks after an awkward moment of us sitting across from each other, neither willing to break the silence. "What they *still* call me?"

"No," I answer softly.

"Monk. Do you know why?"

"No."

"Because the last woman I fucked was my wife before she ran out on me nine years ago," he says calmly, like he didn't just rock me down to my very foundation. "Now, I'm going to go show my daughter what a badass I am at the SeaWolf game. Someone told me it's soul healing, and I think we could all use a little of that tonight."

And then he's gone, chasing after the beautiful little girl we made together in a time when there was nothing but love.

HOUSE UNDERDOGS PROPOSE NEW CONTROVERSIAL BILL

CHAPTER 4

Can't stop

Present Day

"I hate how much I want you."

A hard body presses into mine from behind. The anger in the voice should make me want to run, but I can't, and never could where this man is concerned. I want him more now than ever.

I just had a meeting with Grace, the First Lady. She's adorably pregnant, and everything she wears goes flying off the shelves hours later. Most recently, a pair of maternity skinny jeans and a blouse from Target, of all places. She's since had to trade in her signature Louboutins for a pair of eco-friendly Rothy's flats, but she digs them, and so do shoppers everywhere.

I was walking through the offices when a firm hand grabbed me by my upper arm and pulled me into a dark office. He pressed my front against the dark wall and growled in my ear, "I hate how much I want you."

"I know," I tell him as I press my thighs together. I'm wet and wanting, and we both know it. I shouldn't want him, but I do, and I probably always will.

"I can't see you walk the halls and not feel my cock get hard," he growls.

"I know," I whisper, feeling his hardness press against the small of my back.

"I hate that I need you so much." He skates his hands up the back of my thighs, bringing the hem of my skirt with him. "Tell me you want this. Tell me you want me like I want you."

"I want you," I whine as he pulls my panties aside, and I feel his fingertips brush against my opening. There is no denying how wet I am for him.

"That's my girl," he praises, but I'm not his girl, and I never will be again. I hear the clank of his belt buckle as he undoes the front of his pants and the tear of the foil packet as he protects himself. It's another tragic reminder I can't be trusted to bear his offspring.

I feel the tip of his cock against my pussy, and I arch my hips back to meet him as he thrusts deep inside. I press the palms of my hands flat against the wall and brace against the sting as my body stretches to accommodate him. I bite my lip to keep from calling out and revel in the low groan Rick lets out as it rumbles up my spine.

He places his hands over mine, holding me against

the wall as he begins to move. The push and pull of his body in mine has the air seizing in my lungs. Gone is all semblance of tender emotions; there is no room for them here as Rick fucks me against a wall in a dark office in the White House.

I shouldn't let him. I shouldn't be here at all, with him, but where Rick is concerned, I'm weak. I'll take any scraps he can throw me, even when I know I shouldn't. I should walk away like I did nine years ago. It was better for everyone then, but now I can't stop wanting him.

"I want to hate you," he says, his mouth just barely touching the shell of my ear as he drives deep only to pull back and do it again and again. "Fuck. I want to hate you so much."

"I know," I repeat, my nails scraping against the wall as he pushes me closer and closer.

"But I can't."

"I know."

"Make me," he pleads as he plunges faster and faster. "Make me hate you, so I don't want you so much."

"I can't!" I cry out. I tip my head forward so my face presses against the wall.

His movements become wilder as he loses his tight grip on his control. Each plunge and pull of his cock take me closer and closer to the edge. Just when I think I won't be able to stop the scream that's building with my climax, burning so far out of control that I can't silence it, Rick clamps his palm over my mouth, muffling me as I come.

He drives deep once… twice… before pulling out as he comes.

The loss of him, his cock, his nearness, all serve to sever any connection we made, not matter how fleeting or how toxic. This is clearly a lesson in not having what you want. I want Rick and can't have him. He wants answers I can't give. And somewhere in the middle, we're both left with nothing but wanting what can never be.

I keep my face pressed to the wall, unable to look at him as he slips off the condom and ties it in a knot before tossing it in a wastebasket in the corner. I hear the snick of his zipper as he does up his pants, and then he walks away.

But like I said, I'm weak, so I turn my head, my cheek still pressed against the wall and the back of my skirt tucked up over my hips. All while I watch his back as he walks away from me. That is, until he stops at the door just before he pulls it open, his hand on the doorknob. But he doesn't turn back to face me while he speaks, even as he shatters both my heart and his to pieces.

"I hate how much I want you, and I want to hate you. And I can't seem to stop doing either."

And then he's gone.

RUMORS ARE CIRCLING ABOUT WHITE HOUSE CHIEF OF STAFF AND ESTRANGED WIFE.

Could the Political Mercenary Have Soft Underbelly?

CHAPTER 5

I'll find you

"Mom!" Rachel shouts from her room at the top of the stairs. "Where is my uniform?"

"It's on top of your dresser!" I call back, knowing it's exactly where I laid it out for her last night when Becky's mom called to ask if Rachel could stay the night and then ride to the game with them Saturday morning.

"Thanks, Mom!" I can hear the excitement ringing in my girl's voice. I know it's been hard for her being the new girl in town. But in true Rachel form, she dove headfirst into our new life in D.C., where she would finally get to know her dad.

"Don't forget your cleats!" I call.

"Oh right!" she shouts, making me laugh. While

my girl might dive headfirst into life, she forgets half of what she needs to remember along the way. I pick up her backpack and jacket and hang them in the hall closet before continuing through the house, picking up after my beautiful little tornado.

"Becky and her mom are here," I shout after the doorbell rings.

"Be right there, Mom!"

"Don't forget your toothbrush. No one wants to be the stinky kid!"

"Mooom!"

"Hey, Amber." I smile as I pull open the door, but it isn't Amber and Becky on the front porch; it's Rick.

"Dad!" Rachel screeches like excited little girls do. She's obviously happy to see him like always. And as always, she has no idea what tension lies between her dad and me.

"Hey, wild child." He smiles, coming in and closing the door. "Going somewhere?"

"Sleepover!" she shouts again.

"Ooh, that reminds me," I say, snapping my fingers. "Let me see your bag before Amber and Becky get here. Did you remember your toothbrush?"

"Yes, Mooom," she drawls, handing me her bag just as a car double backfires outside, making her jump. My kid has been raised in cities her whole life, and somehow she's never heard the glorious sound of a car that is about to die.

By some miracle, she has everything she needs right as the doorbell sounds again. Rick beats me to the door, opening it for Becky and her obviously flustered mom, Amber. He smiles his perfect smile at her, and if she weren't happily married, I would want to throw up. But it's the reminder I need. One day, Rick will find someone for real and move on, leaving me behind, just like our story was always meant to play out.

"Hey, Coach Rick!" Becky says as her mom shoots me a knowing look.

"Hey, Amber." I wave.

"Hey, girl, sorry we're late," she says, shoving hair out of her face. "I'm having car trouble again."

"Was that your car sounding like rifle fire?" Rick asks.

"Oh yeah, it does that every time I put the old girl in Park now," she says. "It keeps life exciting."

"How about the new neighbors?" I ask. "Are they interesting? Any cute single men?"

"Oh no," she laughs and Rick growls. "Nothing interesting there. *At all.*"

"That's disappointing."

Amber has become a good mom friend to me as well. We "Wine Wednesday" and gossip about the PTA moms while the girls kick a ball around the backyard. She's asked about Rick a couple times, and I always tell her there's nothing to tell. We're in the past. And we both know I'm full of shit, but she's a good enough friend not to push. Grace, on the other hand, has been giving me crap for months.

"Hey, Becky," he says. "You ready for the game tomorrow?"

"Yes!" she shouts.

"I hear you girls have big plans."

"Yeah! It's going to be so fun!" Becky and Rachel shout together.

"Have a good time," he says.

"Well… I'll just get the girls out of your hair…" Amber trails off before hustling the kids out the door and to her minivan while shooting me ridiculous faces and thumbs-ups when Rick isn't looking.

"Jesus. Are we back in high school?" he grumbles when she finally drives away.

"Amber is harmless," I tell him.

"I like my privacy."

"And yet, here you are at my house," I remind him.

"Can we talk?" he asks me after a moment.

I let out a heavy breath. "Sure, come on in."

I lead the way into the kitchen and pull a bottle of wine from the fridge. I wave it at Rick, silently asking if he'd like a glass too, and when he nods, I pull down two wine glasses. He's clearly planning to stay awhile, and that does not bode well for my night of self-care, where I can indulge in wine, Netflix, and frozen pizza. And if I'm really feeling froggy, the carton of chocolate peanut-butter-swirl ice cream I have hidden in the back of the freezer.

I pop the cork and pour, sliding Rick's across the counter to him. I pick up my own and take a healthy swig. The timer on the oven dings, and I slip my hands into oven mitts before pulling the heavy door down to reveal my dinner plans for the evening.

"Oh my God." He laughs. "Are you still eating that shit?"

"Hey! Don't knock it until you try it."

"I think you fed me enough of it to last a lifetime while we were married," he says, and it's like a bucket of ice water has been thrown over us. We're both thinking the same thing now. How happy we were in the early days of our marriage, and how I cried at the flight-line when I said goodbye, not knowing it was a final goodbye and not a deployment farewell.

"Yeah," I say softly as I lay the pie I no longer want on the range to cool. My belly sours at the memory of how things were left and what could never be.

"Well, it hasn't killed me yet, so another night won't hurt," he says after a moment. Rick is obviously trying to put us back on sturdier conversation ground. Unfortunately, our past is a veritable minefield. I guess I can help him out.

"So you're assuming I'm inviting you to stay?" I tease, knowing he will feel like he can relax again.

"You know you are." He laughs.

"Is that so?"

"You already gave me a glass of wine," Rick argues. "You can't not offer me some of your crappy frozen pizza now. It's like that book *If You Give a Mouse a Cookie*."

"You are ridiculous." I laugh before cutting the pizza into several big slices and placing them on plates. I hand one to Rick and then pick up my own piece, folding it in half and holding it like a giant pizza taco.

"You can take the girl out of Jersey," Rick says, and I turn my head to see him watching me shovel pizza in my face as fast as possible.

"God, this is nothing compared to pizza by the shore," I moan around the bite in my mouth. "I would kill for real Jersey pizza right now."

I pick up my wine glass and take a healthy sip to wash down the slice I just mauled. When I open my eyes again, Rick is watching me with blatant interest.

"What?" I ask and dab at my face. I'm not exactly trying to be cute here. There's probably sauce on my face, because he made it perfectly clear the other day in the offices that he's not going to go down heartbreak road with me another time.

"Nothing," Rick says with a smirk playing about his mouth and a definite predatory gleam in his eyes. "You're cute is all. I had forgotten how much I missed this."

I self-consciously brush a lock of my hair that's come loose from my messy bun back behind an ear.

I don't know what to do when Rick is sweet like this. It scares me so much, because it reminds me of how things used to be, back when we were young and had no idea how cruel the world could be. But that was then, and this is now.

"Come here," Rick growls, his voice low and commanding, and it serves to snap me out of my trip down memory lane. I snap my eyes up to meet his and see his face looks harsh and intimidating under the fluorescent lights of my kitchen.

"W-w-what?" I stammer. My instincts are telling me to step back, to turn around and run, but I don't. Instead, I stay frozen, my bare feet rooted to the floor.

"I said come here." His words are terrifying. This is the political mercenary; my sweet sailor is long gone. I should run, but I take a step forward, and then another, all against my better judgment.

When I'm within reach, Rick hauls me into his arms and crushes his mouth to mine. I cry out in surprise, but it only serves to give him access as he licks into my mouth. I cling to him, my hands caught between our bodies as we devour each other again.

When I pull back to suck in a breath, Rick rips my oversized T-shirt up over my head and tosses it to the floor. I rake my nails down his hard abs and then up underneath the hem of his own T-shirt before pushing it up as high as I can before he reaches behind his neck and grabs the collar to pull it over his head in that sexy way men do.

He glances up at the row of windows that sits over the kitchen sink and looks out onto the backyard. My house is a mirror image of his own that is just next door, so he knows exactly what the view looks like. Most especially because he bought both of the new builds before Rachel and I moved down. But what he sees now, I don't know. What I do know is that the far-away look on his face has me worried.

"Rick?"

He turns his attention back to me but still doesn't say anything. Instead, he pulls me back into his arms, lifting me up by his firm grip on my thighs to wrap my legs around his waist. His steps are sure and even as he carries me up the stairs and directly to my bedroom. When we cross the threshold, Rick kicks the door closed with his booted foot and then proceeds to where my bed sits against the far wall and drops me onto the mattress. I land with a bounce.

"Lie back," he orders as he toes off his boots and socks.

I scramble back on the bed and sprawl out on the pillows in nothing but a pair of bright paisley leggings and a lace bra. Rick opens the front of his jeans with a quick flick of his wrist and pushes them down his thighs, letting his long, hard cock spring free, making my mouth go dry. There always was and always will be something about Rick that checks all my boxes unlike anyone else.

"See something you like?" he asks me, and I can't do anything but nod. "Then I guess we'll have to do something about that."

And then he grabs me by the ankle and pulls me down the bed. I grab onto the white wrought-iron spirals of the headboard to hold myself where I was. When Rick sees me sprawled out like that, there's a twinkle in his eye I don't quite understand.

"I like where you're going with this," he says critically as he pulls my leggings down my legs. Before I can even blink, he's straddling my belly and using my leggings to tie my wrists to the headboard.

"Rick?" I ask, suddenly nervous. There's something about being at his mercy that makes me feel vulnerable and a little uneasy.

Instead of answering me with words, Rick presses his mouth to mine and licks inside, letting his tongue meet mine. When I feel myself melting into his kiss, he pulls his mouth away so he's free to kiss and lick and nip his way down the column of my neck and over my collarbone.

With nothing but an index finger, Rick hooks the top of the lace cup of my bra and pulls it down, bunching the material under my breast and exposing my nipple to the cool air. He gently circles the tiny peak, making me gasp out loud. Stolen moments with Rick are often hard and fast, not slow and sensual.

Rick pulls down the second cup, but instead of his finger, he rolls the tight bud into his hot mouth. I reach for him, wanting to pull him closer to me, but I'm caught in the tangled web he's made out of my leggings and my lies.

He looks up at me as he kisses between my breasts and down my belly, stopping just above my navel. His eyes glitter with excitement and challenge as he watches me pull against my bonds, and I feel his smile pull across my belly.

Rick continues to slither down my body, and I have a pretty good idea of where he's headed. My heart beats faster in my chest, and my palms are slick. It's been a long time since someone worshiped my body like this, since someone took their time mapping every inch of my skin and making me come alive, and that person was the same one pushing my legs wider so he can settle in between them.

"Hey!" I call out when he rips my panties in two.

"You don't need them." He tosses the shredded lace away.

"But I liked them!"

"You'll like this more," he says.

I open my mouth to respond, but before I can speak a single word, Rick steals all thought from my head with a swipe of his tongue up my center. He licks me slow and sweet over and over before finally rolling his tongue over my clit, only to repeat the process all over again.

My climax rolls over me slowly and gently. My inner walls flutter softly, and my skin flushes. I relax against the ties that bind me, thinking Rick will come join me now.

Only, I was wrong. I was so wrong. The sweet, tender evening is over, only I have yet to figure out the rules of the game.

"Tell me why," he implores me in a voice so soft I almost don't hear him.

"What?" I ask, thinking surely he didn't use this moment to manipulate me and my emotions.

"Tell me why you left me," he says just as quietly as he spoke before.

"I can't," I whisper.

"Then again," he says just before he sucks my clit into his mouth and spears my pussy with two fingers.

"Rick," I cry out, but it's no use. His motions are sending sparks shooting all over my body, and as he pumps his fingers in and out of me, I come again, only this time there's a fierceness to it. It wasn't nice, but it was everything I'm feeling in this moment.

As Rick crawls up beside me, I think he's going to let me go, that his game is finally over, but when he leans back and reaches into my bedside drawer, I know it's not, because until this moment, I thought I was the only person who knew what was kept hidden in the back of that drawer.

"Tell me," he whispers harshly.

"You know I can't."

"You can't… or you won't?" he asks as he flicks the black circular cap on the flat end and fires it up.

"What does it matter?" I ask, and I know by the

mean smirk playing about his mouth that we both hear the edge of desperation in my voice.

"Oh but it does matter, Cara." And then he pins my thigh open with his heavy leg when I move to clench mine together. Rick places the buzzing tip of my slim purple vibrator against my clit, and the pressure against my already sensitive place has me rushing over the edge and screaming as I do.

I struggle to slow my heart and suck in some desperately needed oxygen. My muscles ache deliciously, and I know I will feel Rick everywhere come tomorrow morning. I watch with nervous excitement as he kneels between my thighs and rolls a condom down his hard length, gripping himself forcefully in his tight fist.

"Tell me, Cara," he demands as he drapes my thighs over his and touches the tip of his cock against my opening. "Tell me what I want to know."

"No," I whisper, and then he plunges in deep.

My already swollen pussy makes the feel of him deep inside me so much more. Deeper, harder, fuller. It hurts and feels life-altering all at the same time. He closes his eyes tightly for a second as he struggles to get his own body under control, a move I have watched him make time and time again. And then he opens his eyes, and the dark-chocolate brown burns me where I lay.

"Tell me," he says again, and again, I deny him the answers he so desperately wants, but it's for his own good I turn him down.

"No."

"Wrong answer," Rick growls, and then he cranks up the intensity of the vibrator and places it to my clit as he starts to move.

"Rick," I pant.

"Tell me why you left," he demands as he pumps into my body over and over, the vibration burning deliciously against my overly sensitized clit.

"I-I-I can't," I stammer as he burns me higher and higher toward a climax so intense I'm not sure I can survive it.

"Yes, you can," he growls. "Tell me."

"I-I-I—"

"You what?" I'm so close I can't think straight. I think Rick knows this, because he tosses my vibrator to the floor, leaning over me, changing his angle and depth. My breath seizes in my lungs. I couldn't answer coherently if I wanted to as he picks up the pace. "Tell me."

"I-I-I—" I start and then stop to pull on my tether and arch my back to meet his thrusts.

"Yes!" he calls out, and I'm so close. I couldn't stop, even if I tried.

"I did it for you!" I shout as he plunges in again and again. "I did it to protect you."

"What the fuck?" he shouts and pulls out of me, looming over me, and I realize what I've done. What I've said and revealed. And I begin to thrash in my panic.

"Let me go!" I scream as tears burn down my cheeks.

"Never," he whispers, but he still begins to untie me. My leggings are gone, and my hands burn as the circulation starts to flow better again. Rick takes my hand in his and massages it as the blood flows freely again, but I snatch my hand back.

"No!" I shout and scramble to the other side of the bed and away from him. I see the hurt flash across his face before he masks it. "This was a mistake."

"Don't say that," he says as he stands up to walk around the bed to me.

"This is always a mistake," I tell him sadly. "I think you should go now."

"I can't stay away from you," he growls.

"I guess you'll just have to try harder."

"I mean it, Cara," he says, and his voice rumbles with barely restrained anger. And that's okay. It's great, even, because I can deal with anger. I have some of my own stored up too. Anger for our situation, anger for the fact that I'm all alone in my misery, that I have to be the bad guy over and over again. I'm even angry we both didn't get that last orgasm, and it hurts. "I can't stay away, and neither can you."

"That isn't exactly a glowing endorsement to continue whatever this was."

"I'm serious," he warns. "Can you honestly say

you don't want me like I want you?"

"You don't even like me," I say, changing the subject, and it's true. Rick wants me, his cock gets hard for me, and he likes to fuck me, but he doesn't actually like me. I made damn sure of that, didn't I?

"I don't hate you either. And one day, you're going to tell me why you ran," he says softly but with just enough menace behind his words to let me know he's not done, and he's never going to be done until he gets his pound of flesh.

"Don't hold your breath."

I wonder what it would be like to give in, to just let him into my life. I have never heard from the man who threatened Rick and our baby so long ago. Maybe it was just an empty threat? But a strong voice in the back of my head says that it didn't seem so empty when they threatened to have him killed overseas and make it look like he took on enemy fire. They said they had someone close to him on the inside who could get to him faster than I could, and I believed them. I hadn't heard from him in weeks, and it terrified me. I loved him too much to let him die for me. I did then, and I do now. Only now, he has a daughter who has grown to love him and would miss him dearly if something happened to him. So I do what I have to do; I deny the little voice in my head that says I could keep him if I want to, and instead, I push him just a little further away.

"This was always a mistake, Rick," I say softly. I pull in a deep breath before pressing on, flaying the wound open. "It was a mistake ten years ago, and it's a mistake now."

"Don't say that," he says, his voice low and angry.

"We never should have gotten married," I explain. "We were young and dumb and should have known better. And now I think it's time we end this once and for all."

"Do you now?" he asks as he crosses his arms over his chest. When he put his jeans on, I'll never know, but as I finally look at him now, I see he's ready to leave and not naked and bare like I am.

"I do." I nod. "I won't be at the soccer game tomorrow. You have that time with Rachel. I will see her tomorrow night when she gets home."

"Fine," he clips out, his jaw tight.

"Fine," I repeat.

"I see you're scared, and you want to run, but know this," he warns. "If you do, if you run from me again, I'll just have to track you down and fuck it out of you. And I will find you. I have more resources, and I'm not tied down to an enlistment contract this time."

"Rick—" I start, but he's already gone, and my bedroom door slams behind him, followed shortly by the front door. And as I lay there, naked in my bed, feeling my body used in a good way and also bad ways too, I let the tears roll unchecked down my face and think my life couldn't possibly get worse than this.

It's too bad I would find out later how very wrong I am.

PRESIDENT OPENLY
OPPOSES NEW BILL

CHAPTER 6

What happens in Vegas

"L*et's do it.*"

Rick and I are naked in his bed. Our legs are tangled together, and he keeps twisting a lock of my hair around his finger over and over again.

"What?" I ask, distracted. Rick has a way of making all thought fly out of my brain with just a look or a touch. I'm so wrapped up in this man that it's ridiculous. I am so in love with him.

"Run away with me," he whispers on a smile before he presses his lips to mine.

"I already did, silly," I tell him the truth. This trip was not planned, but after I met him in a bar on the east coast a few months ago, we haven't been able to stay away from each other. So when he asked to buy me

a plane ticket to San Diego for a little sex on the beach before his next deployment, I said yes in a heartbeat. "I flew to California at the drop of a hat for a booty call."

"Is that all this is to you?" he asks me seriously. "A booty call?"

"No," I whisper softly. "And you know it."

"I do," he agrees, folding my hand in his and pressing it against his chest. I can feel his heart beating rapidly in his chest. "So marry me."

"What?" I ask, surprised. That's crazy, right? We've only known each other a few months. And we live on opposite coasts. This can't possibly work.

"I know what you're thinking," he says quickly. "And it is crazy, but it's not. If you really think about it, you know we're meant to be together. You're meant to be mine."

"What about my life on the east coast?" I ask, not that there's much tying me down there. I have no family left.

"You can go to school here and move when you're ready," Rick answers. "I'm going to be gone for a while, but I'd like you to be here when I get back. As my wife. So what do you say?"

"Yes."

"Yes?" he asks, a huge smile spreading across his face.

"Yes," I answer him. "I'll marry you."

"You're mine," Rick says as he rolls me to my back.

"I'm yours," I repeat just before he slides in deep.

I wrap my arms and legs around him and hold on tight as he slowly rocks in and out of my body, bringing us higher and higher together. And it's together, in each other's arms, that we fall over the edge.

Rick and I hold on to each other; we breathe each other in. I have never felt this close to another human being before. I am Rick's, and he is mine, and there will never be anything that will tear us apart. Yes, this is crazy. No, we haven't known each other for very long. But in my heart, I know Rick is the only man I am ever going to love, and I know without a doubt there will never be another. And the way Rick holds me just as tight tells me he feels the same way about me. It tells me everything.

"What do you need?" he asks me when our hearts slow and breathing evens out.

"Not a thing," I answer him honestly. "Just you."

"What about a dress?" He toys with a sweat-dampened lock of my hair near my temple.

"It's not important." I shrug one shoulder, because in the grand scheme of things, it's not. It's just a dress.

"I thought every girl dreamed of their wedding dress," he says thoughtfully. Rick is always thoughtful where I'm concerned. He is so attuned to me and my needs that it's uncanny.

"I'm not every girl."

"Don't I know that," he growls before rolling me to

my back again and grinding his hips into mine. "Other girls don't make me this hard."

"I thought you wanted to get married?" I ask him and giggle.

"I do." He sighs before sliding from the bed with his regret written all over his face as if he didn't just come ten minutes ago.

"I think you'll survive," I tease him and then squeak when he grabs me by my ankle and yanks me out of bed. "Rick!" I shout as he throws me over his shoulder and runs to the bathroom.

"I think you'll survive," he mimics my words as he steps under the freezing water of the shower, and then I really scream, making him laugh.

"You are a dead man, Rick Donovan!" I shout as he soaps me down.

"And you're about to be a very happily married woman."

"You're just lucky I love you so much," I say before he shoves me under the frigid spray again to rinse off. "And you're good in bed."

"I love you too."

"You better," I snap, even though I'm clearly enjoying myself watching him soap up his body as I inch as far away from the cold water as possible.

"Oh, I do." He winks at me before giving his cock an extra stroke and a squeeze for my benefit.

"Why are we taking a polar bear plunge right

now?"

"Because my dick could drive nails right now, and you so helpfully reminded me that we have a wedding to attend," he says, eyeing his dick and then looking pointedly at me.

"What did I do?" I ask, wondering what I did to earn the glare and the cold shower.

"You make the dick hard," he says like I should know the answer.

"You should control it better," I tell him. I can barely get the words out before I'm laughing so hard my belly hurts and I can't catch my breath.

"Oh, you think this is funny, do you?"

"Maybe." I eye him suspiciously.

"Then you'll find this hilarious," he says just before he hauls me into his arms and crushes his mouth to mine.

And then we were an hour later leaving San Diego than we had originally planned.

"I DON'T NEED a dress."

"You need a dress," Rick presses as we walk

through another shop in the Forum.

"I don't." I let out a frustrated sigh before looking down my body. I'm in a flowy, white eyelet tank and frayed denim shorts. Brown leather flip-flops show off the coral nail polish on my toes. I don't look any worse than Rick, who is wearing tan cargo shorts and a gray T-shirt that displays his ripped forearms and the frog feet tattoo on his inner bicep.

"You do," he says with more feeling than I would have thought a dress warranted. "I want you to have every girl's dream, but I can't get you that on short notice, so I want you to have a dress and flowers and a ring. I want you to remember today as the best day of your life, free of regrets."

"I think this one is nice," I say, pointing to a white tea-length dress hanging on a rack after I swallow the huge lump in my throat. "Besides, I already have every girl's dream, because I have you."

Rick pulls me into his arms and kisses me long and deep, his tongue sweeping into my mouth and leaving me breathless. It's over far too soon. And then he plucks the dress I've chosen off the rack, the hanger looking small and delicate in his large hand before he turns back to me.

"What else?"

"Shoes," I tell him before walking over to a wall of heels and selecting a box in my size.

"What about the hat thing that covers your hair?" he asks, making me laugh. Rick always makes me

laugh when I need it most, reminding me what's really important.

"A veil?"

"Yeah," he answers me. "That. But don't cover your beautiful face. I like to look at you."

"This one." I grab a bag with a picture on the front that looks like it fits the bill. "I think that's it."

Rick takes all my selections up to the register and pulls out his wallet, paying for them. The saleswoman looks disappointed that it isn't a bigger sale, but I think this is perfect. I don't think I would want anything fancier than this. I have never dreamed of what it would be like to have a big wedding with a dad who looked proud to walk me down the aisle. Mostly because I never knew my dad. When I was eleven, my mom died, and then I was all alone. I wasn't mistreated, and for the most part I was pretty lucky with how it played out, but even in the best scenarios, the foster care system isn't the place for fanciful dreams.

"So now that I have a beautiful dress and you're in shorts and a T-shirt, how is that fair?" I ask, laughing.

"I packed my dress whites," he answers. "I want everything to be special for you."

"It is," I whisper, feeling suddenly choked up.

"No, but it will be," he says before grabbing my hand and leading me to the next shop, where he buys us matching gold bands.

And then Rick leads me back to our suite in the

Paris Hotel that overlooks the Eiffel Tower and the Strip. I sit at the dressing table, curling and pinning my hair and touching up my makeup so I look like a bride, while Rick showers.

I strip out of my shorts and tank and pull on the white lace panties and matching longline strapless bra. I place the clip of the veil above my chignon and arrange the fluffy tulle behind me before unzipping my dress and pulling it from the hanger. I step into it and pull the zipper up my back as far as I can, but the back remains open.

"Shit," I bite out, not noticing the water had been shut off until I feel warm hands slide into the opening of the dress, tracing my spine.

"Can I help you?" His voice rumbles in my ear.

"I can't get the zipper all the way up," I admit.

"Well, let's see what we can do about that," he says.

I regret the loss of his hands on my back when he slips them from my dress before expertly sipping it up. When I look back at him, I see his crisp, white uniform with his perfectly rolled neckerchief and a ton of medals on display. He cuts a striking figure of pure masculine perfection.

"Thank you," I tell him, letting my fingers slide across the brightly colored ribbons and medals before stepping into the shimmery nude heels on my feet.

"I'm not gonna lie," he says, his voice sounding rougher than before. "I'm going to prefer taking it off

you more."

"Me too," I whisper before shooting Rick a saucy grin over my shoulder. "We should go before we miss our appointment."

"Now we wouldn't want to go and do that," he says on a cheeky grin before putting his white sailor hat on his head and pulling open the door for me.

Rick holds out his arm for me, and I take it, letting him escort me into the elevator and then down to the valet and cab lines. A yellow cab pulls up when it's our turn, and Rick holds the door open for me before sliding in beside me.

"To the Little White Wedding Chapel, please," he says to the cabbie before taking my hand in his.

Rick silently toys with my fingers while we ride to the chapel. I look down to where they sit intertwined with his on his muscular thigh, when I feel the cool metal slide down my ring finger. A slim gold band with tiny diamonds all around it glitters on my finger, and it's the most beautiful thing I have ever seen. It's also not one of the plain gold bands we bought today.

"I wish I could give you something bigger, fancier, but this is all I could afford right now—" Rick starts to explain the beautiful token of his love as if it's not enough, when it's so beyond anything I ever dreamed of. I can't let him keep going, so I interrupt him, placing my free hand on the side of his jaw and pressing my mouth to his.

"It's perfect. I love it."

"I'm glad." He smiles just as the cab pulls up to the front of the chapel. "I would give you the world if I could."

"You already have." Just then, the cabbie opens the door and we step out onto the curb.

"You must be Rick and Cara," an older man dressed like Elvis in the rhinestones and cape phase says, and I barely hold in my amusement. Rick's eyes twinkle with merriment. I'm glad my dress has pockets and my credit card is stowed away, because we're definitely going home with the photo package now.

"Yes," he answers. "We are."

"Excellent. Right this way." Elvis leads us into an office at the front of the chapel, where he takes Rick's credit card and hands me a small bouquet of pink roses and baby's breath tied up in a black satin ribbon.

"Thank you," I say as I smell the sweet roses and wonder what I could have done in this life or the last to deserve a man as loving and wonderful as Rick. He is everything I could've ever wanted and then some.

"Right this way," Elvis says, leading us into a small sanctuary where he stands at the podium and picks up a small binder. He looks very official for an Elvis. "You may take her hand."

An older woman with a camera snaps pictures, and we smile and pretend she's not there as Rick takes my hands in his. The way he looks at me makes me feel like I'm the only woman in the world. I can only hope I make him feel this special. Fortunately, I'll have every day of the rest of our lives to prove it to him.

"Dearly beloved," Elvis begins, "we are gathered here today to unite Cara Cataldo and Richard Donovan in holy matrimony."

Rick doesn't take his eyes off me through the entire ceremony. I love you, he mouths the words, and I whisper them back. The moment is so beautiful it's seared on my heart.

"Rick, do you take this woman to be your lawful wife, to have and to hold for all the days of your life?"

"I do."

"Cara, do you take this man to be your lawful husband, to have and to hold for all the days of your life?"

"I do."

"Rick, please place the ring on Cara's finger and repeat after me."

Rick slides the solid gold band down my finger to sit next to my diamond band. "I give you this ring as a symbol of my love and faithfulness. As I place it on your finger, I commit my heart and soul to you. I ask you to wear this ring as a reminder of the vows we have spoken today, our wedding day."

"Cara, place the ring on Rick's finger and repeat after me."

I slip the ring down past his knuckle and speak from my heart, hoping he hears how important these words are to me. "I give you this ring as a symbol of my love and faithfulness. As I place it on your finger, I commit my heart and soul to you. I ask you to wear this ring as a reminder of the vows we have spoken today, our wedding day."

"And now, by the powers vested in me by the State of Nevada, I now pronounce you husband and wife. You may kiss your bride."

Before Elvis ever speaks his final words, Rick sweeps me into his arms and dips me back as he crushes his lips to mine. It's as if he was waiting for those little words to be spoken before he could act, and he waited so patiently. Almost.

Elvis and the older woman chuckle at our passionate display that is over too soon. She gives us a card to collect our photos tomorrow, and Rick leads me out into the night while they throw rice at us.

It's by far the best day of my life, and as I look at Rick as we run out into the Vegas night, I know it will only get better from here.

**MATERNITY
JEANS WORN
BY FLOTUS AT
SOUP KITCHEN
SELL OUT IN
MINUTES.**

CHAPTER 7

"Hello?" I pull out my phone from my jacket pocket and answer.

I'm sitting at a small desk in Grace's offices. She has a few important events coming up that she has to be styled for, so I'm pulling ideas from various designer catalogues online. She's risen so high in popularity that everyone is watching what she wears, even if it's just to the gym. And I love the clothing budget. I have definitely given Jake's black AmEx a workout lately, and he couldn't care less.

"What a pretty little girl you have," a robotic voice says after a series of clicks and beeps. And the altered voice takes me back to another time and place. Even though I can't recognize it, in my heart of hearts, I know who it is.

No. This can't be happening. I worked so hard; I

have sacrificed so much, all to keep the monsters at bay, but somehow, they followed me home after all.

"Who is this?" I demand. I refuse to believe this is happening again. It can't be. The unfairness of the situation hits me like a slap across the face.

"You know who this is," they answer after a heavy pause that has my stomach sinking into my toes.

"I did what you said," I say in a broken whisper. It feels like all the blood has drained from my face, and I feel lightheaded. The only thing keeping me grounded right now is the knowledge I have to stay strong for Rachel. "You said you would leave me alone if I did what you asked, and I did."

"She looks so happy playing in the schoolyard," the voice says. "So carefree and innocent. She has no idea the things her parents have done."

"No," I whisper, looking around to make sure I haven't drawn anyone's attention. "I don't believe you."

"That's a lovely blue ribbon in her hair."

"No." The sob that threatens to rise up from my chest is audible in my whispered protest. I know if I can hear it, he can too.

Rachel was just given that hair bow by her new bestie Becky over the weekend. Becky's mom, Amber, made matching bows for the girls of bright blue ribbons mixed with soccer-ball-patterned ribbons. But she hasn't had it long, so whomever this is, is watching her now.

"It would be such a tragedy if something happened to her. She has her whole life ahead of her…" the voice trails off, but the threat is there. It's like a living, breathing thing that stands between us. And I know without a doubt he will follow through on his threats if I don't tread carefully.

"No!" I cry. "I've done everything you've asked. Leave her alone. Please. Just leave her alone."

"Have you?" the voice prompts. "Have you really done everything I asked you to? Or are you connected to Donovan again? If memory serves me, he was the price you so happily paid. Well now the stakes have been raised."

I am. Rick is back in my life, and now we are more intertwined than ever, even more so than when we were married. Something told me when Rick crashed back into my life that I was dancing with the devil himself, but I had stupidly ignored the feeling. I left Rick years ago to protect him, and now I'd have to leave him again to protect our daughter. And I will.

I have always loved Rick, and it's been physically painful being near him and not having him completely, but I would give it all up again to protect Rachel. Rachel is my everything. She is the best of both of us and has her whole life ahead of her. What happens to me no longer matters; my pain is no longer relevant, and neither is my joy, because she is everything.

"I'm sorry," I whisper. "I made a mistake."

"You know what to do." And then the line disconnects.

My stomach roils at the thought of a creep watching my baby. I have to get to her now. I can't be away from her any longer. Every second that ticks by is another that could mean total devastation. It's the middle of the school day, but I don't care. I'll check her out and take her home to hunker down for movies and Chinese food. She'll love it. I have to keep her safe. And hopefully, she will never know the wolf was knocking at our door.

I scoop my keys up off the desk and log out of the computer I was using. My heart is pounding so fast it feels like it will beat right out of my chest. My palms are slick with sweat, and my brain is swirling a mile a minute. My thoughts are racing with so many what-if scenarios, and I can't make it stop. I sling my pocketbook over my shoulder and run out the office door and right into a hard body. Thick arms banded with heavy muscle close around me, and full lips brush my ear.

"Hey, baby, I was just looking for you," he purrs in my ear.

What I wouldn't give to go back and be able to lose myself in his body. To be ignorant in the unfairness of our situation, of the rules of the game and the die that had been cast against us.

God, how I would have loved to hear those words spoken like this a month, a day, an hour ago even, but now, I can't. I can't have anything to do with Rick Donovan, because it could very well cost our daughter her life. Oh how I would trade places with her in a heartbeat. A life for a life. Mine for hers. I would do it too. Without hesitation. She would be safe and happy living with Rick, and I would be gone.

Whatever monsters I brought into their lives would be gone forever with me.

"I have to go," I whisper, and my voice sounds wrong to my own ears. His body stiffens in response, and I know he hears it too.

"Cara?" Rick asks. I can hear he's on alert, looking for the threat and where it might come from. "What's wrong?"

"Nothing. I just have to go." I try to push away from him, but he tightens his arms around me. No. Why can't he let me go? I just need to go.

"Tell me what has you spooked," he pushes. "I need to know what happened."

"Nothing happened," I lie, even as my voice shakes and we both know it's not true. "I'm fine. Everything is fine."

"I told you that I was done letting you run," he growls in my ear. "Whatever shit you've spun up in your head, you better tell me now, and we can work through it, fuck it out, whatever you need to get the fuck over it."

"Thank you for reminding me we're better off apart," I say tartly. Somehow, Rick always manages to bring out the worst in me. I know that's not fair to put it all on him, but holy fuck, I need to get out of here, and he chooses now to fight this out? This is why we shouldn't be together!

"We are not," he growls, sending shivers up my spine. I knew better than to poke the bear, and I did it anyway. Some days, I wonder if I will ever learn.

"We are," I reply. "Can you honestly think this is the way loving parents should treat each other? That we're setting a good example for our daughter by engaging in this toxic of a relationship?" When he's silent, I press on. "You can't, can you? Because there is nothing healthy about this. I don't want to be treated this way."

"You didn't seem to be complaining when I was dick-deep inside you Saturday night," he growls.

"You're good at it." I shrug. "Can you blame me? But that doesn't mean we should carry on the way we are."

"So that's it?" he snarls. "You're scared, so you're going to run again?"

"Yes," I answer him, because this needs to be over sooner rather than later, so I can get to Rachel as soon as possible.

"You don't need to run anymore," he pleads, and I can't bear to see the look in his eye while he lays himself emotionally bare at my feet. "I'll protect you from whatever has you running scared. Even if it's your own damn self."

"We can't keep doing this," I tell him. "It will only hurt Rachel in the end."

"Two parents who love each other and love her won't ever hurt her. And you know it."

"You don't know that," I snap. Fuck! Can't he see I have to go? This is wasting time I don't have.

"Cara—" Rick starts, but I don't let him finish it.

"I have to go," I tell him one more time as I push away, and this time, he lets me. Thank God.

"This isn't over," Rick warns me.

"Just stay away, Rick."

I walk away from him, and as I move down the halls, I hear the spoken word "Never" bounce around me.

And oh if only that was how it could be. But girls like me don't get the fairy-tale endings.

WHITE HOUSE CHIEF OF STAFF HAD SECRET DAUGHTER

CHAPTER 8

Mu shu cluster fuck

"Mom?" Rachel asks when she walks through the doors to the front office of her school.

"Hey, honey," I say, pasting a fake smile on my face. If anything, I can't let her feel how hysterical I am on the inside.

"They said I have a dentist appointment?"

"I got done with work early and thought we could play hooky for an afternoon," I whisper my lie in a conspiratorial fashion.

After I left the offices like a bat out of hell, I knew I raised more than a few eyebrows. Tomorrow, I'll tell them all I started my period and had to leave quickly. Nothing like getting photographed by the paparazzi with blood-stained clothes. That should explain away my strange behavior. I jumped in my car and raced all the way to Rachel's school. It felt like it took forever to get here, but really it was just shy of twenty minutes.

I walked into the office and told them I thought with all the recent changes that had been made to Rachel's life, she could probably use an afternoon to decompress and have a little fun with her mom. I told them to tell her she had a dentist appointment until I revealed our plans for the rest of the day. The ladies in the front office of this school are the best, so they were more than happy to play along.

"Are we going to get into trouble?" she asks.

"Of course not, darlin'," the older lady who works the front desk says with a happy smile. If only she knew the thoughts that drove me to come here and spirit away my only child; she might have more reservations about the situation.

"Oh okay." She slings her backpack high up on her shoulders and follows me through the parking lot and to my car. I do my best to hide the fact that I keep looking over my shoulder like a teenaged shoplifter. I feel a nervous tingle up the back of my neck, but when I look for signs of anyone watching us, I see none.

"How does Chinese sound?" I ask when I slide behind the wheel of my little Jeep.

"Mu shu chicken?" she asks, looking so hopeful I know what's coming next. "And ice cream sundaes after? Pretty please? With a cherry on top?"

"Yes." I laugh as I pull out into traffic. "Dial up

the Golden Dragon and order. We'll swing through the grocery store on our way, so it'll be ready when we get there."

"On it!" she cheers as she jumps into action. I love that my girl is such a happy child. Her zest for life is amazing. "Should I text Dad and ask him to come?"

"Oh… uhh," I start to panic all over again. The way I left things with Rick this afternoon was not a happy one. And I need him to stay away in order to keep Rachel safe. "I think I remember something about him having a late meeting tonight."

"Oh okay," she says, sounding sadder than before as we pull into the grocery store's parking lot.

"Let's go get all the candy," I tell her with a big fake smile.

"And whipped cream and cherries!" she says, catching on to my subject change.

"Absolutely!"

I beep the locks of the car behind us, and Rachel grabs a cart from the rack by the front door on our way in. We like to pretend we're on *Supermarket Sweep* when we come in for snacks and junk food. It's weird, but it's fun. It's just our thing.

I let Rachel get a little carried away as she tosses in different kinds of ice cream, frozen pizzas, cold cereal, and candy. Chips and juice as well. I wouldn't usually let her choose all the things, but I throw in fruit and vegetables when she's not looking. This will keep us covered if we have to hunker down for a while, while I figure out our next moves.

"Having a party?" the cashier asks as we load up our haul on the conveyor belt.

"Yeah, something like that," I mumble while Rachel happily chirps about her favorite boy band on the cover of *People Magazine*.

"So do you, Mom?" she asks me.

"Huh? What did you say?" I ask, shaking my head from side to side like that will clear my thoughts. My daughter shoots me a look that says she is not amused I wasn't paying attention to her, and I hate that I wasn't.

"I said, 'Do you think Uncle Jake will invite Sudden Drop to the White House, and then I can meet them?'" she asks me, making me laugh.

"You know you can't use your connections to the president for your own personal gain, right?" I ask, taking over loading the groceries into the cart before I pay the cashier and start pushing it out into the lot.

"Ugh," she whines. "You're no fun. I'll ask Dad." And the thought of the terrifying Rick Donovan being the fun parent makes me laugh.

I unlock the car before handing her the keys. "Why don't you get in the car and lock the doors while I load the groceries."

"Why?" she asks, scrunching her brow while she works out the pieces of the puzzle that don't fit. She's just like her dad that way.

"Just to be safe," I answer a little too quickly. "This

isn't the best neighborhood. I'll be done in a second."

"Okay," she says, eyeing me suspiciously before taking my keys and climbing in the car. I breathe a small sigh of relief when I hear the locks click and then toss the groceries in the back as fast as I can.

I knock on the window, signaling for her to unlock the doors, which she does with a "You're so weird" muttered just loud enough for me to hear. I slide behind the wheel and quickly relock the doors before taking my keys from her.

I drive to the Golden Dragon, a restaurant Rachel and I found and fell in love with when we first moved here, largely because of their crispy wonton noodles and red eggroll sauce they give you in massive quantities with your order. I take a few more turns than were necessary, and I know Rachel notices. She could do this drive in her sleep if she wasn't only eight years old.

"Mom?"

"Yeah, honey?"

"Where are you going?" she asks me.

"To the Golden Dragon."

"But why are you going this way?"

"Oh, I just thought I'd try something different," I lie.

"Oh okay."

I pull into the parking lot and cut the engine. Rachel and I jump out of the car right as it begins to rain, even though it was sunny two minutes ago. Weather on the east coast is so weird. I may never get used to it.

She grabs my hand in the parking lot like she does in every lot, and I secretly love that she still does. I hate and love equally every rite of passage she meets. We race into the restaurant where we are greeted with smiles and hugs by the owners, an older Chinese couple who have adopted Rachel and me. I wonder if Rick is treated the same here or if he's just another patron.

I slip her my credit card while her son, who has been asking me out for over a month now, carries our bags out from the kitchen for us. Rachel and I take them quickly, and I make excuses about groceries in the trunk, so he won't ask me out again. He's good-looking and funny and so sweet. But I am so still in love with my ex-husband. Maybe my life would be easier if I just dated someone like Aaron, but that's not fair to him, to me, to Rick. So I will just be alone until Rick moves on.

We grab our bags of takeout and rush back out to the parking lot where we climb in and buckle up. I start the car and we head home. Rush hour hasn't quite started yet, so the roads are not very busy, and it doesn't take us long before we're pulling into the garage.

"Why don't you go inside and pick a movie while I get these groceries?" I ask her. "And take dinner in with you and put it on the coffee table."

"Okay, Mom!"

I grab as many bags as I can from the trunk and follow her inside before dumping them all on the island in the kitchen. I head back out to the garage and grab the last load. When I get into the kitchen, the groceries from the first load have already been put away, and I can hear my daughter puttering around upstairs.

I finish tossing the pizzas and ice cream in the freezer before running upstairs to change into a pair of yoga leggings and a tank top. When I make it back downstairs, Rachel is dressed in her own brand of comfort clothes—a pair of running shorts and an old oversized T-shirt she stole from the back of my closet. It's faded gray from too many washes, but you can still see the bold letters across the front that spell out NAVY. She had jacked it from me, and I had stolen it from her father. The irony is not lost on me.

"What's all this?" I ask when I see her laying out a feast fit for a king. "There's no way we'll eat all this. Did we get someone else's order?"

"Uhh…" she hedges just as there's a knock at the front door.

"I wonder who that could be."

"I… uhh… I kind of invited Dad," she admits, and I look back at her, noticing the table is covered with not only our favorites but Rick's too. "Don't be mad."

"I'm not mad," I say just as Rick lets himself in.

"Everybody decent?" he calls out.

"Yeah," I answer. "We're right here."

"I see that," he says. "I thought this was dinner. Is

someone dying?"

"Very funny." I roll my eyes.

"Oh, God," he whispers before eyeing me nervously and then his daughter like she's a live bomb. "Did she uhh…. Did she start?"

"Start what?" I ask, not understanding what he's trying to ask me. There are too many things on my mind right now to focus.

"Her period," he whispers harshly.

"Oh! No, this isn't that. We just like to gorge on takeout and watch movies from time to time," I answer. "I thought it was just going to be us. She kind of sprung you on me."

"I would apologize if I was sorry, but I'm not," he says, making me smile.

"I know."

"Are you mad?" he asks me.

"No," I answer honestly, even though I'm freaking the fuck out.

Maybe there's another solution to my problems. Maybe Rachel and I could move back to New Jersey, and then Rick would only be in our lives from time to time. But his words from last night ring in my ears. I know that if I try to run again, I won't get very far. Nine years ago, we were young and dumb, and Rick was fairly newly minted to the teams with only a few missions under his belt. Now, he has the resources of the most powerful man in the world accessible to him at his very fingertips. I have no doubt that if Rick asked, Jake would rain hell on me to get his friend's daughter back for him. And to be honest, if I were in his shoes, I would do the same fucking thing.

"I love this movie!" Rachel says like it's a war cry as she queues up the *Trolls* movie.

"I can't wait," Rick says with a gentle smile for his only child, and the moment is so tender and sweet, but I still can't help the smirk that curls up the right corner of my mouth, because this poor man has no idea what he has just gotten himself into.

"Great choice, sunshine girl." It was also the only choice. Since the movie came out, we've been listening to the soundtrack in the car and singing at the top of our lungs whenever humanly possible. She also watches the movie on repeat.

"What's that look for?" Rick asks me suspiciously.

"Oh no reason."

I grab my plate and load it up with mu shu chicken roll up in the little dumpling wrappers, fried rice, and crispy wontons. I scoop up my chopsticks and sit back so I can watch Rick enjoy his evening.

Rachel scoops up a paper carton of orange chicken and a pair of chopsticks to dive in. She spins them around her fingers like a drummer in a hardcore marching band and then dives in. I smile proudly, because I taught her that move, and it's nice to see her enjoy it.

"Those are some slick moves, princess," Rick compliments her.

"Thanks." She beams at her father. "Mom taught me."

"I know," he replies before turning a pointed look on me. "I remember the move well."

I shouldn't love that he remembers all the little things about me that he does, but I do. A shiver wracks up my spine as his dark-hazel eyes heat just a little. And I love it all. So I curl up in the corner of the sofa and pick at my dinner, wondering if I'll have any heart left when I walk away from him one last time, because I have to. Whether he lets me or not, for Rachel's safety, I have to find a way.

Rick picks up a container of steamed chicken and vegetables with no sauce or rice. It's the same thing he always used to order. He would laugh when I scrunched up my nose at the boring choice, telling me that his body was a temple, and from the glimpses I've had of him over the last few months—most of our sexual encounters, he stays mostly clothed—it still is. Where I have softened around the edges with pregnancy and then life, Rick has stayed hard-bodied, ripped abs and all, and it's bullshit.

This time, it's his turn to smirk when he understands where my mind has traveled when he catches his disgusting dinner choice in my direct line of sight. He knows I love his body, and I always have. But it can't go on like this. So I silently force out a heavy sigh and then eat the rest of my feelings and mu shu.

When the movie is over, Rachel quickly clicks over to *Pitch Perfect*. And I want to laugh at the look on

Rick's face. I don't. I come close, but I find some restraint.

"Something funny over there, pretty girl?" he asks me.

"No, not a thing," I answer before moving my hand across my chest in an exaggerated X. "Scouts honor."

"So when does old Dad get to pick a movie?" he asks, and Rachel shoots him a look that would make mere mortals cower. I like to think she gets that look from him, like it's coded in her DNA.

"Why?" she asks suspiciously. "What would you pick?"

"I don't know… *Braveheart, The Patriot,*" he suggests. "No?"

"Uhh…" I laugh. "Don't you think those are a little bloody for an eight-year-old?"

"Umm…" he says, looking uncomfortable, and I want to put him out of his misery.

"Ice cream time!" she shouts before pausing the movie and running into the kitchen.

"Don't worry, Dad," I say softly. "She'll be ready for your brand of entertainment before long. Now let's go gorge on ice cream."

"How about you?" he asks softly, his husky voice just loud enough for me to hear. "Are you ready for the brand of entertainment I have planned for you?"

I swallow back my nervousness audibly and don't agree or disagree. I change the subject like a chicken-shit. "I think I'm ready for ice cream."

"Sure," he says, smiling that wicked smile that reeled me in like a big mouth bass on day one. "I'll let you have that play. For now."

I make my way into the kitchen and feel Rick's steps follow me. His heated gaze could burn a hole through the ass of my leggings, and the moisture pooling between my thighs reminds me that I will never not want him.

"Holy fu—" he bites out as he takes a look at all the crap Rachel and I bought at the store earlier when I was distracted. My lack of parenting skills is piled up on the island for all and sundry to see.

"Whoops," I admit. "We might have gone a little overboard at the store earlier."

"You think?"

"I was distracted, and the tiny powerhouse I birthed took advantage of me in a weak moment," I protest.

"You're the parent," he grumbles, and it's not quite loud enough for Rachel to hear, but all it takes is one look at her face to know her confidence with her dad is slipping.

"We have an audience," I say out of the side of my mouth. "Smile."

"So where do we start?" he asks our daughter.

"Ice cream," she answers, clearly realizing his displeasure was with me and not her. I made a point to talk to her when he entered her life, and I told her that sometimes grownups disagree. It is never, not *ever*, her fault and that no matter what, we both love her more than anything in this world.

"Sweet."

"That's the idea." I wink.

"Mom likes half a banana in her bowl," Rachel says, side-eyeing me. "I do not."

"I would love to split a banana with Mom," Rick says, snatching one up from the hammered copper bowl on the counter and peeling it with his nimble fingers. Fingers I know all too well what they're capable of. He breaks it in half and hands it to me with a knowing smirk, the bastard.

I take it and break it into chunks with my hands before dumping them into my bowl. I scoop out my favorite chocolate ice cream, and Rachel passes me the chocolate syrup. We have created an art form over the years of ice cream sundae assembly. When we're done, we high five each other with our spoons and then look at Rick, whose bowl contains half a banana and one scoop of plain vanilla. To be honest, I'm not even sure where the vanilla came from, because Rachel and I wouldn't waste our time on that shit.

"That's it?" I cry. The words are out of my mouth before I can stop them.

"Uhh… no?" he asks before carefully shaking out three plain M&M's into his bowl. Plain! I shake my head at him and then walk back into the living room.

We resume our places from earlier, and Rachel

picks up the remote, pressing Play on *Pitch Perfect.* We eat more ice cream than we probably should; well, Rachel and I do. I'm not sure Rick has ever had ice cream before. I hope his stomach can handle all that rich dairy and sugar. I cringe thinking he might have a long night ahead of him, but it doesn't look like he actually ate more than the banana.

We laugh through the movie, even Rick. And I will admit, it's one of my absolute favorites, and I love that my daughter loves it just as much. We sing along most of the time, but this time we both seem to enjoy Rick getting to see it for the first time. I wonder, not for the first time, what his life has been like since I left. I know he hasn't dated, and I know he had never seen *Pitch Perfect* before tonight. But I can't help but wonder what he did for fun.

It's late by the time the movie ends. Rachel is sprawled on the length of the sofa like a college coed after their first frat kegger. She does this so often on movie nights that it doesn't even faze me anymore, but the look on Rick's face when he notices her is one I will never forget. The way his face gentles, she brings out a softness in him that I thought was long gone. And if I thought he was sexy before, seeing him as a good dad is earth shattering and devastating all at once, because he is everything we should have had if it wasn't taken away from us like it was.

"Can you help me get her upstairs?" I ask. "She's getting too big for me to carry anymore."

"Of course," he says, and I can hear him try to clear

the emotion from his voice.

"Thanks," I reply, leading the way up the stairs. I don't look back to see him scoop her up like a newborn baby and hold her with all the reverence a first-time parent feels when they hold their child for the first time. I can't. I know it will shred my heart, and I have to guard that organ fiercely so I can protect our daughter in the coming days.

I pull back the covers of her bed, and he gently puts her down, and I cover her up. I pretend not to notice when he lets his fingertips trail gently over the threadbare baby blanket with the little blue anchor stitched in the corner folded up next to her pillow. When he stands up, I smooth her hair back from her face and walk out of the room, flipping the lights off as I go. Rick stops in the doorway and looks back at our daughter, who is sleeping peacefully in her bed like she doesn't have a care in the world. I've protected her from the monsters outside her entire life, and I would go to hell and back to keep her safe.

Failing is not an option.

I walk back downstairs and start gathering up bowls from the coffee table. I dump them all in the empty dishwasher and then start putting away our junk food fest in the fridge and cupboards. Rick silently helps. He doesn't ask; he just dives in and starts putting things away. The task is done in no time at all, and now I'm left with a frustrated Rick, who is prowling like a tiger when I need to put distance between us.

"Well," I start awkwardly, "thanks for the help."

"So that's it?" he asks after watching me for a long length of silence. "You're just going to dismiss me?"

"No," I lie. "That's not it at all."

"Then tell me what it is?"

"It's late, and I have to work in the morning and get Rachel to school…." I trail off.

"And that's different than any other night we've spent together since moving here how?"

"Rick… this has been a mistake."

"Bullshit," he roars.

"A beautiful mistake but we're both headed for heartache here," I tell him, which is truer than anything I've said tonight.

"Maybe I'm already there." His words hang in the air between us like a ticking time bomb. Everything is about to explode. I can't have him in our lives, because the results could be catastrophic, but I can't figure out how to keep him away either.

"No," I whisper.

"I'm in love with you, Cara," he says, stabbing his fingers through his dark hair. "I have always been in love with you."

"You can't," I plead. He doesn't know how dangerous his words are, but I do. He has to stop. This has to end.

"I do. I think I always have, and I know I always will," he says, stalking toward me. "I know you'll never tell me why you left, and I'm at peace with that. I know you're spooked now."

"Rick—"

"Hell, I'm scared too. If anyone has the ability to crush my heart, it's you," he says, cornering me. He's backed me through the kitchen and into the living room. The backs of my legs hit the arm of the sofa. "But I refuse to let you run away this time.

"Rick, you have to let me go."

"Give me one good reason why," he says softly. Rick bends his knees so that he looks into my eyes instead of down on me.

"You know I can't," I whisper.

"That's not a good enough answer anymore," he says gently, and then he touches his mouth to mine. He kisses me so softly, so gently at first that I almost can't bear it.

"Rick—"

"Let me make you feel good," he pleads, and I think, *Why not? What's one more time?* "Let me love you.

"Yes," I whisper, and he kisses me again, breaking apart only to pull my tank top over my head, leaving me in only a white lace bralette I like to sleep in. Things aren't as firm or as high as they used to be before I had a baby.

There's a hint of a playful look on his face that I can't decipher right before he places his hand at my belly and gently pushes me back, over the arm of the sofa, making me laugh. But I don't laugh long, because he shucks his T-shirt over his head, giving me a much-wanted glimpse of those washboard abs I love so much.

My breath is sawing in and out of my lungs by the time he grabs the waistband of my leggings and panties and pulls them both down my legs in one swift motion. I bite down on my bottom lip as the cool air hits my overheated skin.

I hear the clank of his belt as he loosens it before letting his jeans fall to the floor, where he steps out of them. He grips the base of his cock in his fist, and I watch with rapt attention as he strokes himself from root to tip once… twice… and then a third time before he puts his knees to the sofa cushions in between my spread thighs.

He lets go of himself to lean over me, bracing his weight on his arm over my head. Rick presses his mouth to mine, his kiss everything we want to say but can't… or shouldn't; I don't even know which anymore. All I know is this moment is ours. It's for us to make up for all the years we've lost and all we won't ever have.

He lets his fingers trail down my body, between my breasts, and over my belly before letting them slip even lower to part my center. Rick gently slips inside me, and I lift my hips to meet his gentle thrusts. He skims my clit with his calloused thumb, making me gasp. Every inch of my body flushes hot and is centered on the one spot where he touches me.

Rick watches me with unwavering focus, his dark

eyes never leaving mine even as he adds a second finger, slowly filling me over and over again while he gently abrades my overly stimulated flesh with his thumb.

"Rick," I pant as I reach for him. "I need you."

But he gently kisses my palm and returns it to the sofa next to me. "No, Cara," he says softly, never stopping my deliciously slow torture while he pushes me closer to an orgasm one tiny inch at a time. "You know what I want you to give me, and I want it all."

"I need you," I plead. I want to feel his cock deep inside me when I come. If this is going to be our last time together, I need to be joined with him in the most basic of ways, even if it's just for a moment.

"I know what you need."

And then he curls his fingers inside me as he presses down on my clit harder than before, making me see stars. I close my eyes, my body bowstring tight, and then I come with Rick's name a whisper on my lips.

He covers me with his body then, the tip of his hard cock poised at my entrance, and with his eyes still locked on mine, he slides deep.

If I thought this would be a hard and fast fuck, I would have been wrong. Totally fucking wrong. There's something about tonight; we're both racing the clock against fate. She's a cruel bitch, and we both know it. Tonight is about showing each other how we feel. It's about showering each other with the love that can never be spoken out loud.

Rick lays more of his weight on me, and I wrap my

arms and legs around him. I would happily take all of it. I need to feel him like this. I need so much tonight. He slides his arms underneath mine and holds my head in his hands. I feel so delicate, so cherished in his arms, and I always have. Even when he hated me, I felt special in his arms, but it was nothing like this.

He touches his mouth to mine, breathing me in, touching, tasting, and I blossom underneath his kisses. He licks into my mouth, but it's not aggressive; it's gentle and sweet. His nose brushes against the side of mine.

And then he begins to move.

Slowly, oh so slowly, he slides in and out of me, making a torturous pattern back and forth where our bodies are joined. I hold him tighter in my arms, silently begging him to fuck me, but he won't relent. Rick knows what he wants, and he's not giving in.

We hold each other tight, drinking each other in as he plunges in over and over. Our bodies rock together in a delicate dance just for us, and if I could live in this moment forever, I would be tempted to try.

"Rick," I gasp and dig my heels into his ass, begging him to move faster, harder, but he only smiles against my mouth, keeping his maddeningly slow pace. He arches his hips, changing the angle and deepening his penetration. "Yes."

Finally, he moves faster. He is still gently gliding in and out where our bodies join, but now he's moving faster, hitting a spot deep inside me that has my toes curling into the soft fabric of the sofa.

He thrusts deeper still, and I dig my nails into the backs of his shoulders. My body burns hotter while he pushes me to soar even higher. And finally, when I can't take anymore, he drives in one more time, sending me over the edge.

"Cara," he gasps as he follows behind me into bliss.

Rick drops his forehead to rest on mine while we both work to catch our breaths. A fine sheen of sweat coats both our bodies, and I can feel his heart beating just as wildly as mine is.

This was a beautiful goodbye. Poetic even.

This was the most excruciatingly beautiful goodbye that could ever be shared between two people who love each other as much as we do, and it will haunt me for the rest of my life.

"Marry me," Rick whispers, his sex-rough voice breaking the eerie silence.

"Wait, what?" I ask, knowing there is no way I could have heard him correctly.

"Marry me," he says louder this time. "Again."

"No," I whisper.

"Yes," he implores me. "Marry me again. Let's be a family. A real one."

"No," I say. "You don't know what you're asking for, and if you did, you wouldn't be asking."

"Well I am," he snaps. "This is right, and you know it."

"It isn't," I cry as I push at his shoulders. He relents and sits back on his knees, his cock slipping from my body, making me feel cold and empty. "This can't happen. You don't understand."

"Then make me understand," I hear him say through my rising panic. Tears slip free from my eyes. "I love you," he adds, and it sounds both sweet and menacing all at the same time.

"I know."

"And I know that you love me too."

"I know that too," I whisper, the devastation in my voice laid bare for both of us.

"Then marry me."

"I can't." I barely push out the words before I choke on a sob that rises up from my chest before I can even try to stop it.

"I should have known you'd say that," he bites out as he stands and shoves his legs in his jeans. He buttons them and buckles his belt faster and angrier than I thought possible of anyone. He stabs his arms through his T-shirt after scooping it up off the floor, yanking it down over his head. "This is far from over."

"We have to stop this, Rick," I plead. "It hurts too much."

"I just fucked you bare, Cara," he says, and I feel shock give way to horror as the emotions shift like old vacation slides across my face. He was so meticulously careful and it had felt like a punishment of sorts every time he slid a condom on, like I couldn't be trusted not to run off into the night with another one of his children and now he throws caution to the wind. The night had gotten away from us, I was there, I know. And Rick wouldn't try and trap me like that. But he damn well could have anyways. "I see you get it now. If you think I'm going to let you go again. With a baby in your belly. Again. You've got another think coming."

"We don't know that anything happened." I try to get the train on the tracks as he stalks toward the front door.

"Wrong fucking answer, Cara," he bites out. His own hurt and anger are riding him hard. "We're in this now, and there's no way out until we see this through. I can promise you that."

"No," I whisper as the ramifications of Rick's resolutions play through my mind one after another, but he doesn't give me time to explain.

"I guess we'll see about that."

And then he's gone, the front door slamming behind him, and I'm left trying to rationalize how I can feel both elated and terrified all at the same time. And to what end? Who will pay the price for my dance with the devil? Because if it's Rachel or even Rick, I know I won't survive it.

Fortunately, or unfortunately, depending on how one looks at it, I wouldn't have to wait long for the other shoe to drop.

RUMORS OF
DISSENTION
AMONG WHITE
HOUSE
STAFFERS HEAT
UP

CHAPTER 9

Taylor Swift's "I Knew You Were Trouble" blares from my nightstand, making the pulse pounding in my head so much worse. I clench my eyes closed and blindly slap around for the offending piece of metal and glass. Once it's firmly in my hand, I crack one eye open and hit the button to stop my alarm. I feel hungover, but it's not alcohol that made me regret my life choices. It was a man and a badly broken heart. And the worst part is? I did the breaking. Again.

I thought the song was ironic, given my tumultuous relationship with Rick, but now it just hurts. Maybe he's not the one who's trouble; maybe it's me.

After Rick slammed my front door behind him, I quickly scooped up my clothing previously discarded in a sex fueled haze and made a break for my room. I

can't imagine anything being more awkward than being caught in a walk of shame by your eight-year-old
child. I know I'm not a perfect parent, but that feels
like it crosses into bad parenting territory.

I had shut my bedroom door behind me and dumped
my clothes into the hamper before pulling on a T-shirt
and a clean pair of panties. I pulled the covers back on
my bed and climbed in. And only when I was safely
tucked in the thick covers did I let the rest of my tears
fall. I cried for Rick and for me. I cried for Rachel and
the life she should have but will never get to know.
I cried for all the friends I've made and will have to
leave behind. They will never forgive me for what I
have to do in the morning.

I swing my legs over the side of my bed and sit up,
and then I rub my hands over my eyes and hope the
blinding pain behind them will ease if even just a little
bit. And then I push up from the down-filled softness
that calls to me to stay and sleep away the day, but
that's not fair to Rachel. That's not being a good mom.
Even in the early days before she was born, I never let
myself wallow. I always put one foot in front of the
other, because it was always for her.

I make my way into the bathroom and turn the taps
as hot as I know I can stand it. I strip off my T-shirt and
panties and catch the last traces of Rick on my skin
before I toss my clothes into the hamper. I step into
the shower and let the water and steam envelop me.
I'm tempted to cry some more and really feel sorry for
myself, but Rachel can't be late for school, and I can't

be late for my meeting with Grace.

I wash quickly and then shut off the taps. I notice I smell like lavender and vanilla like usual now as I grab a fluffy towel from the rack and wipe the droplets from my body. I make my way into my closet and pull on a matching bra and panty set and then slip my favorite tank dress off the hanger. It's olive-green with cream stripes, and the best part of all is the hidden pockets. I slide my feet into tan leather ballet flats, the heel of the working mom, and slip a pair of gold hoops onto my ears.

I make my way back into the bathroom and twist my hair up into a messy ballet bun on top of my head and do a five-minute makeup routine of soft pinks and golds. Sometimes, it's nice being a pro. I know how to look good in less than ten minutes, which is a life-saving skill, because I am always running late.

I quickly head down the hall and knock on Rachel's door. I push it open and see her blink her eyes against the early-morning sun.

"Morning, sunshine girl." I smile at her.

"Morning, Mom."

"Get dressed, and I'll have breakfast waiting for you downstairs," I tell her before making my way down the stairs and to the kitchen.

I quickly down more than the suggested amount of Advil and half a pot of coffee before I start making sandwiches and packing lunches. I make sure Rachel's backpack is packed, with her jacket hanging over her pack on the hook, so it's all easy for her to see when she's ready to leave the house.

She rushes down the stairs right as I'm pouring her a bowl of Cheerios, and I smile against the clanging in my head the sound of the cereal filling the bowl causes.

"Yes!" she cheers. "I love that cereal."

"I know you do. That's why I buy it." My kid is weirdly healthy most of the time, our Chinese takeout and ice cream feast nights notwithstanding. I'm pretty sure she gets that from her father too. Lord knows, I love a good pizza. "Eat quick. We gotta run."

"Okay," she says before diving into her breakfast while I sip my coffee.

When she's done, she races upstairs to brush her teeth and then races back down again. She's kind of like having a really busy puppy. Her uniform polo is hanging out of her tan shorts in clumps, making me laugh.

"I think you need to fix your shirt," I tell her.

"Why does it have to be tucked in anyway?" she grumbles. "Uniforms are dumb."

"Uniforms are supposed to 'level the playing field,'" I quote the information pamphlet on the private school she attends, making her laugh. "Plus, you love your new teachers and friends."

"I know," she concedes. "And I like being near Dad." My heart pangs. She doesn't know we'll be leaving soon. She's going to hate me for it, but when she's older, I hope she understands why I'm going to do what I have to.

"Grab your stuff," I tell her. "We gotta hit the road."

Rachel slips her jacket on and plucks her backpack from the hook by the door to the garage. I hit the button to open the overhead garage door and lock the door to the house on my way out. We climb into the car, and I pull out of the driveway and head toward the fancy prep school Rick was able to secure midyear for our only daughter.

She's not a morning person at all. When she was in preschool, Rachel would routinely put herself back to bed when I woke her up in the morning. But this morning, she's more subdued than normal.

"Mom, are you mad at Dad?" she asks.

"No!" I answer quickly. "Why would you think that?"

"Well, last night, you said he couldn't come to dinner, and then after, you guys were weird," she says, shrugging. "I don't know."

"We're just learning how to be parents together," I explain. "I've had you all to myself for eight years now, and Dad just wants to get to be in Rachel's world too."

"I like that," she says as I pull into the drop-off line at her school.

"I thought you would." I smile back.

"I love you, Mom!" she says just before she throws

open the door and jumps out.

"I love you too! Have a good day." And then one of the teachers smiles at me before shutting the door that my daughter forgot to close when she saw one of her friends and took off.

I spend the rest of my commute wondering how I'm going to tell my best friends I need to leave. I can't tell them the truth, but I also can't be cruel. I wish I could tell Grace and Jules what's really going on, but then Grace would want to involve the president, and involving Jake would mean involving Rick. And that's a risk I just can't take.

I park my car in the staff lot and badge in through the marines guarding the staff entrances. I smile and thank them for scanning my purse and then make my way down the hall. I'm almost to my little office amongst the first lady's staff spaces, when I see Rick stalking down the hall like an angry tiger. I duck back into a little alcove.

"Have you seen Cara?" I hear him ask someone.

"No, I haven't," they reply. "I'm sure she'll be here eventually. Is she supposed to work today?"

I am, but I'll call in sick if it means avoiding Rick for another day. Although he lives next door, so I'm sure that won't help matters. Rick will just come over when he's tired of being avoided.

"She must have hit some traffic," the other guy says. "I have a meeting. I'll see you around."

"Yeah," Rick says absentmindedly. "I'll see you

around."

I stay hidden in my spot until I hear footsteps trail away. My heart is beating so loud in my ears that I'm surprised I could hear them over it. My phone buzzes in the oversized hobo bag on my shoulder. Thank God I keep it on silent or it would have given me away. I pull it out of my purse and feel my stomach plummet to my toes.

RICK: Where are you? We need to talk.

I don't even unlock it. I just read his terse message on the lock screen. I don't want him to get a Read message and know I know he's looking for me and I'm hiding somewhere. Unfortunately for me, another message buzzes before I can drop the offending phone back in my bag.

RICK: I know you're here. The marine on duty told me you checked in.

Oh good, now he's using the White House Security Detail to keep tabs on his ex-wife. *Real classy, asshole.* My heart pangs in my chest even though I'm irritated with him for his invasion into my work life. I still hurt. I want to be near him. I would run to him and tell him everything if I could, but it's just not safe.

RICK: I have to go into a meeting. Everyone is waiting on me, and the look Jake is giving me now is not making me happy.

Thank God he's going to be occupied. Hopefully, I can get in and out before he's done with his meeting. I'd like to be long gone. Hopefully the president is feeling longwinded this morning.

RICK: You better be in your office when I'm done here.

I am not going to be anywhere near my office by the time he's done. With any luck, my daughter and I will be halfway to Canada by then. Or Aruba.

RICK: If I have to hunt you down, I'm going to be pissed. But I WILL hunt you down.

Good luck with that. I drop my phone back into my purse and make my way to my office, which by another miracle is as far away from Rick's as it could possibly be. It'll take him a hot minute to get to me, and I'm going to be gone by the time his meeting is over. Rick can try to find me, but I've gone to great lengths before to stay away from him and to protect our daughter. I'd do it again.

I let myself into my office and lock the door behind me. My nerves are too frayed this morning to be bothered by anyone. I'm struggling to keep my mask in place today, and if anyone saw me, they would know that everything is wrong. And then they would tell Rick. In hindsight, the fact that everyone is all too happy to tattle on me to Rick should have been a major red flag.

I push out a frustrated sigh, sit down at my desk, and fire up my computer. Grace has a state dinner, a school visit, and a tour of a new battered women's shelter she will need to be styled for. She's so fun to dress, because not only is she gorgeous, but she has incredible taste and a flair for fashion, while being known as accessible and down to earth in her Louboutins. Well, she was until Jake made her give them up the more visibly pregnant she's become.

I would love making these outfits on a regular day, but today, my heart just isn't into it. I send links to the outfit pieces I want her to consider in an e-mail. Because she has such a great sense of style and what works for her body type, it doesn't take her long to make a decision. I chose an emerald-green flowing chiffon gown for the state dinner. It has a sweetheart neckline and cap sleeves of the sheer material and a black satin belt that will show off her growing bump to a T. For the school visit, a baby-blue maternity dress with cream-colored polka dots and nude leather ballet flats. And for the shelter tour, a black-and-white polka dot maternity blouse, black jeggings with black leather ballet flats, and a winter-white hip-length coat.

I think she's going to love them all and they will be a go. The two more casual outfits are ready to wear and already in my online cart in her sizes, but it's the gown that will be a little more difficult. Not really. It's by a local designer who loves to dress Grace. All it takes is a quick text message, and he'll have the dress in a garment bag and halfway here to pin it to her.

But when I pull my phone out of my bag, I see the notification for more text messages. I must not have heard it in my bag. I know Rick is irritated, but not this angry. In time, he will see this is the way it was always meant to be.

Only, when I open my text app to message Xavier about his green dress, I see the latest messages aren't from Rick at all but from a blocked number. My heart races as I tap the word UNKNOWN, where a number should be. I shouldn't open it; I know I shouldn't. Only bad things can come from this message.

UNKNOWN: You should have listened.

My breath saws in and out of my lungs and not in a good way. It feels like I can't get enough air as I read the warnings and look at the picture that followed.

UNKNOWN: [PICTURE]

It's a photo of Rick and me on my sofa last night. We're both naked except for my bralette I was wearing. My eyes are closed and my head is tipped back in ecstasy. You can see all of the tension on display in Rick's honed muscles. The veins in his neck are exposed, and his teeth are clenched tight.

I quickly type out a reply before it's too late.

ME: I did what you asked. I ended things.

It feels like my heart seizes in my lungs while I wait for a reply.

UNKNOWN: Not soon enough. You should have listened to my warning. Now it's too late.

My fingers type furiously. I grab my bag and scoop up my things while I wait for a reply. I have to get to Rachel before it's too late.

ME: NO! It's not too late. I did listen. Rachel and I are leaving this afternoon. We're getting out of town and will go far away.

I don't even bother to shut down my computer or turn off the lights. I'll send a message to security from the road. I don't have time to waste on menial tasks. I'll e-mail Grace from wherever we are tonight and say goodbye. Apologize.

UNKNOWN: It's too late.

No, it can't be. I'll get to her before it's too late. I have to.

And then the video comes through.

UNKNOWN: [VIDEO]

I press Play, even though I don't want to. I have to. The thumbnail is a picture of my daughter looking scared and worried.

"Mom," she says. "Mom. I'm scared. I need you."

UNKNOWN: You should have done what I told you to.

And then my vision dims and my knees buckle. I hold on but barely. Everything I sacrificed was a waste. Without Rachel, I have nothing.

There's only one thing left to do. Without knowing it, this monster just changed the rules of the game. I have nothing to hide now.

Checkmate, motherfucker.

FLOTUS HEADS UP POWERFUL 'GIRL TRIBE' INSPIRING FEMALE FRIENDSHIPS

CHAPTER 10

Nothing left

Nine years earlier...

I can't help the smile that spreads across my face as I walk through the baby section at Target. In my basket is the cutest little baby blanket with an anchor stitched in the corner and matching little baby socks. Whether it's a boy or a girl, they're going to use this blanket no matter what. I am so proud of their daddy, and I will make sure they are too.

This morning when I woke up, I puked my guts up, just like I did yesterday morning, and the one before that. I brushed my teeth, threw on some running shorts and a tank, and headed for the PX that's around the corner from our apartment. I grabbed the first pregnancy test my fingers could touch and paid for it before jumping in my car and heading back to the apartment to take it.

I didn't even read the directions. I mean, how hard could it be? Step one: Pee on the stick. Step two: Wait the longest three minutes of your life. I had set my old-fashioned egg timer. I chewed on the cuticle of my thumb nail the entire time it ticked away. But when it finally dinged, I held my breath and looked down to where it rested on the bathroom counter.

Two pink lines peered up at me, and I knew that in a few short months, it would be Rick's gorgeous dark-hazel eyes that peered up at me from the face of our child. And I could not wait. Being married to Rick is a dream come true. He is loving and considerate. He even calls as often as he can from overseas. And I know he will be a great dad. This is all a fairy tale come to life for a girl with no family who grew up in foster care. I've never had anyone or anything, no people to call my own, so having an amazing husband and a baby on the way—what more could I ask for?

I carry my little red shopping basket over the crook of my arm as I look at baby bottles and pacifiers, onesies and little caps. I let my fingertips glide over a gray wooden crib, and I'm instantly in love. Boy or girl, this is the crib; I know it. I'm excited about it all, and I can't wait to tell Rick when he calls home tonight.

I decide I should probably pick up some prenatal vitamins and a quart of milk before I check out, because I'm out at home. I walk through the pharmacy section and choose a bottle of vitamins in a happy pink bottle and then head to the dairy section. I'm scanning the aisle for milk and pick up some little cheddar bites in a bag and drop them into my basket when my phone rings. I don't recognize the number, and I wonder if Rick was able to call sooner than he thought he would.

"Hello?" I answer quickly.

There are a series of pops and clicks before a robotic voice speaks. I'm about to hang up, and then he says my name. "Don't hang up, Cara."

"Who is this?" I ask. I'm not playing games with any telemarketers today. Nothing is going to ruin my mood.

"You're going to get a text in a second," the voice says. "Look at it. And know that I'm serious."

"Serious about what?" I snap as I reach for the milk in the cooler. My fingers curl around the handle and I pluck it from the shelf.

"Serious about the fact that I will have your precious husband killed if you don't do exactly as I say." The milk slips from my fingers and crashes to the floor, exploding all over. "I see that I have your attention now."

"Yes," I whisper.

Ding! My phone's text tone chimes, making me gasp.

"That'll be the message now," the voice says.

UNKNOWN: [PICTURES]

I open my text app. It's picture after picture of Rick and other sailors and soldiers in various uniforms on some base in a desert. I don't know much about where he is now, because he couldn't tell me, and I was okay with that. I understand my place as a military wife.

He looks happy in some. I always know he loves what he does. He's smiling at something another man is saying to him.

"I don't understand what this means," I say after I raise my phone back to my ear.

"It's to prove to you that I have access to him, and if you don't do as I say, your husband will die in a friendly fire accident before the day is through," the voice warns.

"No."

"Yes," they hiss like a snake.

"What do you want me to do?"

"I'm glad you're finally listening." They chuckle, but I do not find one thing funny about this situation.

"What do you want me to do?" I ask again.

"Leave him."

"W-what?" I gasp. I couldn't have heard correctly.

"You're going to hang up the phone and go pay for your groceries," the voice says, and I look over my shoulder, wondering who it is I'm talking to. They laugh again. "Don't bother; you'll never find me."

"Why are you doing this?"

"That's not for you to know."

"What am I to know?"

"Nothing other than what I'm telling you to do

right now," the voice says. "Buy your items, go home, pack your bags, and after you tell your husband good-bye when he calls, you leave and never look back."

"He will never believe me."

"Then I guess you better make it believable. Or else you won't like the consequences."

And then he hangs up.

I look down at my phone and flip through the pictures of Rick, and in my heart of hearts, I know this is the last look of him I will ever have. I place my free hand over my still flat belly. I don't know how I'm going to make this right for us, but I will. We're going to be all right. Because we have to be.

And then I do what I was told. Only I don't select another quart of milk, because I won't be home to drink it. I take my purchases to the counter and put them on the conveyor belt. The cashier takes one look at my baby socks and blanket and my copy of What to Expect When You're Expecting and guesses right away.

"You're having a baby," she says with a sweet smile.

"Yeah," I whisper.

"What a blessing. Congrats to you and your husband."

If only today had gone the way it started out, with so much joy and promise, but now it's nothing but survival and heartache with some terror thrown in for fun.

"Thanks," I reply. I pay for my purchases and head

for my car.

I pull out of the parking lot on autopilot. I head to the apartment and let myself in. I don't take my purchases out of the car; I don't need to. Instead, I pull out the duffle bag from the closet and fill it with a handful of clothes. I don't even care what I grab, just enough to get by. Nothing has meaning anymore.

And then I sit on the sofa in the late-afternoon sunlight and wait. I don't turn on the television or any lights; I just sit there and wait until the sun starts to set and Rick calls.

"Hi," I say when the Skype call comes through.

"Hey, baby." He smiles that panty-melting smile I love so much. "I miss you."

"I miss you too," my voice cracks.

"Hey, what's wrong?" he asks, and his voice is so full of concern that I can't take it.

"Nothing," I start and then I shake my head. "Everything. I can't do this anymore."

"What?" Rick breathes. "I don't understand."

"Then I guess you better make it believable," I hear the robotic words over and over in my head. I have to make Rick think this is believable, even as I break my own heart right along with his.

"I can't do this anymore, Rick." Hot tears burn down my cheeks.

"What are you saying?"

"I don't want to be a Navy wife anymore. I don't

want to be married."

"What?" he asks, and shock is written across his face.

"I'm not cut out for this," I tell him. "I don't know if I was ever meant to have a family of my own. Maybe I was always meant to be alone."

"You don't mean that," Rick says. "Baby, just hear me out. We'll get through this together."

"No," I cry. "We can't. I won't be here when you get home."

"Don't say that!" he shouts.

"I'll have an attorney send papers to you. Just sign them and move on."

"No!" he barks. "I won't."

"You can do better than me, Rick," I say sadly. I feel broken inside. "We both know that."

"No, I don't know shit, and neither do you," he says in a tone of voice he's never taken with me before now.

"I do," I sob. "I've always known. Be safe, Rick. And be happy."

"I won't be happy without you," he pleads, and me neither. I won't be happy without him, not ever again, but I'll exist for my baby. That's all I can do now. And Rick will live to see another day, to marry again and be happy, all because I'm walking away. "I love you, Cara."

"Goodbye, Rick." And then I end the connection before whispering, "I'll never love anyone but you."

And then I slip off the rings he was so proud to give me and I loved so very much, and I leave them on the coffee table along with the sim card to my cell phone so he can't find me. I grab my duffle bag and my car keys, and I just drive. To where or what, I have no idea.

I have absolutely nothing left.

But this baby will have me, and that's going to have to be enough.

POTUS AND
FLOTUS TAKE
MIDDAY LUNCH
DATE. HEARTS
SWOON AT THE
ROMANCE

CHAPTER 11

Taken

Present day…

I know exactly what I need to do. Or really, who I need to go to. If this was another time and place, I would appreciate the irony of the situation—that this morning I was avoiding him, hellbent on running away, and now I'm running to him.

I clutch my phone in my hand so tight I'm afraid the glass will shatter, and then where will I be? I had just stopped the video. I'm going to be sick, but I can't now. I have to get to Rick. If anyone can fix this, it's him. I know we have a lot to atone for between us, but I also know I can trust him with this.

My lungs burn with the air that isn't filling them as I race from my small office in the First Lady's offices to the presidential offices.

"Stop, ma'am," one of the marines who guards the offices says. "No one is allowed back here."

"I need to see Rick Donovan right away," I tell him as I flash my badge. My voice is thread, and my hands shake. "It's an emergency."

"Right this way, Ms. Donovan," Gus, one of Jake's Secret Service agents says from somewhere behind me, surprising both the sentry and me. Granted, I'm a little jumpy right now. "You can wait in his office. I'll tell him you're here."

"Can't I just go to him?" I ask. "It's important."

"No, ma'am," he tells me gently. "He's in a closed-door meeting," Gus explains.

"Oh okay," I say. "Just… please hurry."

I pace Rick's office while I wait for him. If he doesn't show soon, I'm going to puke in his waste-paper basket. My stomach is turning over and over. Sweat beads my upper lip and my hairline. The room swirls around me while I struggle to get my bearings. The offending video on my phone plays in my brain on a loop.

These things are time sensitive, right? And my baby. I can't bear for her to be away from me for one more minute. I need to get to her, but I don't know where she is. I left her safe and sound at school just a few hours ago, and now she's just… gone.

"What the fuck could be so important that you've interrupted me during a closed-door meeting, Cara? Did you break a nail?" he seethes. I know he probably hates me again after my refusal of marriage last night. I hate me too. I did things he will never understand to protect him, to protect Rachel, and now it was all for nothing.

"She's go—" The words get stuck in my throat, and I can't get them out.

"Who's gone?" he asks, his body instantly alert.

"Our daughter," I explain, holding out my phone with the video queued up. "Somebody took Rachel."

"Our daughter," I explain. "Somebody took Rachel."

And poor Rick. He just found her, and now if something happens to her, it will gut him. I know he hates me, and I accept that he should, but Rick is a good man and an even better father than I could have dreamed he'd be. He is the way he is because of me and my actions, not because of him or who he is deep down.

"What do you mean somebody took Rachel?" Rick asks after a pause.

"She's gone, Rick," I answer in a panic. My belly is churning with acid and I know I'm going to be sick just saying the words. "Someone took her from the school."

I hold out my phone with the video queued up. Rick takes the little stack of glass and metal that hold our whole entire world in them.

Rick takes the phone from my outstretched hand and I watch as he hits play, his face is blank until the video starts and I watch the tightening of his jaw, his fingers whiten around my piece of shit phone, it's the only outward sign he gives that he's upset. Rick is a fortress and I'm that little piggy's straw house, one more gust and I'm toast.

I clench my eyes tight and will the sounds of our daughter begging me to come get her away, but I can't. I can only use them to harden my heart and steel my resolve to find her by any means possible.

"I think I know who did it," Rick says after a moment. He still doesn't look at me; he just continues to scroll through the messages on my phone. He sees everything, and I'm okay with that. For the first time in almost ten years, I'm not hiding anything from him, and it feels so much better.

"You do?" I ask, surprised. How could he know who did this? But even if he does, this is good. We can get her back right now. "Well, go get her. We have to get her back."

"I'll get Rachel back if it's the last thing I do," he vows. God, I hope it's not. He and Rachel need time to get to know each other after spending almost nine years apart. I don't want anything to happen to either of them. I love them both, and I always have. If we get through this, maybe we'll finally have our chance at the family we were denied years ago. But it's too soon to let myself hope now. Now, I have to do whatever Rick says we need to.

"Please," I beg. I hope he knows I mean I need him to get our daughter back but also need him to come back in one piece as well.

"I don't know exactly who it is, but I think I know *why*."

"What? Why?" I question. I don't understand. Why would someone want to hurt our little girl? Who could do something like this?

"Someone is trying to blackmail the president, and the only way to get to him is through me."

And then I drop to my knees and promptly throw up in the wastebasket after all. I feel a handkerchief blot at my hairline before his strong hand gently grips my chin and turns my face toward him so he can wipe the corners of my mouth. It reminds me of how tender Rick could be when we were first together, before I ruined everything.

"Thanks," I whisper. My face heats with embarrassment as I realize the sexiest man I've ever known just watched me toss my cookies.

"I think it's time we have a serious talk, Cara." Rick's voice is low and rough as he warns me there will be no going back from this.

"I know."

"No more lies," he warns me.

"I know that too."

And then he grips my upper arms softly, he holds me delicately, like I'm fragile, and helps me to my feet. But the sweet way he cares for me ends when he lets his hand slide down my arm to hold tight to my hand,

and then he leads me to the gallows.
It's time to face my judgment.

IS THE PRESIDENT AS SQUEAKY CLEAN AS HE CLAIMS?

CHAPTER 12

Someone is always watching

"I need you to do something for me, pretty girl," Rick says, lifting my chin to face him, making me cringe. "It's going to be really hard, but you have to do it.

"W-what's that?" I ask, knowing in my heart of hearts that he's right. Whatever he's going to ask me to do is going to be really hard, but then again, everything for the last nine years has been, and for my daughter, I'd walk through fire, so bring it on.

"There's my fighter," he whispers as he looks over my features. Whatever he sees in my face, he approves of.

"Whatever it is, I can do it."

"I need you to pretend like nothing is wrong."

"Except that," I tell him. "I can't do that."

"Cara," he says, and I can tell it is with great patience that he does so. Ironic, because I'm about to lose mine.

"I'm serious, Rick," I snap. "Our daughter is missing."

"I know that," he explains. "And we're going to find her. But right now, the kidnappers think they have you in their pocket. That you're afraid—"

"Because I am afraid."

"So that you'll continue to do whatever they ask of you," he finishes. "So you have to pretend like nothing is wrong. Business as usual."

"But I can't," I breathe. Doesn't he know that acting is not in my nature? I avoided him instead of pretending like nothing was wrong, and he saw through my bullshit the entire time. So will the kidnappers.

"You have to, because someone is always watching, Cara," he rationalizes as he holds up my phone in his hand. "These pictures and messages prove someone is always watching you and me both. Not to mention our daughter."

"They said I broke the rules, but I didn't," I tell Rick, hoping he'll believe me. That I didn't just throw all regard for our daughter out the window. "I told you to stay away."

"I broke them, honey, and for that I am so sorry," he tells me. "I couldn't let you push me away. I accepted Rachel's invitation to dinner. I came back knowing you were trying to push me away again, and I didn't want it. I wanted in your life and in Rachel's. I didn't give you a chance to say no."

"I knew better," I cry.

"I know," he says gently. "But we don't have a time machine. We can't go back and change things now. We can only go forward."

"Okay," I say. "What do we do?"

"We're going to get her back, but right now, we have a lot to talk about." I nod in acceptance, because he's right. We have a lot to clear the air. And I will do whatever we have to in order to get Rachel back. Rick clearly likes whatever he sees on my face, because he nods and says, "Let's get out of here."

And we do.

LOOKS LIKE NO LOVE
IS LOST BETWEEN
CHIEF OF STAFF AND
EX-WIFE. ROMANCE
SHIPPERS
HEARTBROKEN

CHAPTER 13

Time to call in the cavalry

"Are you ready?"

"Sure," I answer, and as soon as the words are out of my mouth, I know I'm not ready. Rick kicks open the office door so hard it slams against the outside wall.

"Get out," he growls.

"W-what?" I stammer.

"I said get the fuck out," he commands as he grabs my upper arm like a criminal and marches me through the building. "I know just what to do with a coldhearted bitch like you."

"Rick," I whisper, but he stops me from speaking when he turns to me with a harsh look plastered over his handsome features.

"I've heard enough out of you," he says to me, and

it feels like a kick to the stomach.

He marches me out of the building and back through security. I hang my head low so they can't see my face. Hopefully, they just assume I'm sad or that Rick finally caught me in whatever it is he thought I was doing. It's honestly not too far of a stretch. Everyone who works around us—and hell, even the press—have been speculating about Rick and me for the last six months or so. Things had gotten so heated, the rumors so wild, that I bet they would believe anything at this point.

Rick marches me through the parking lot. He pulls his keys from the front pocket of his slacks. The lights flash and the locks open with a beep when he hits a button on the key fob. He yanks open the passenger door with more force than necessary, and I cringe.

"Get in," he barks at me, and my body folds into the front seat against my volition. It's as if I didn't have any other choice than to follow his terse commands. "Buckle up."

And then he slams my door before stalking around the hood to the driver side. And then he pulls open his door and climbs in. I scramble to pull my belt across my body and buckle it when Rick shoots me an angry look as he buckles his own seat belt and throws the car in Reverse, backing out of his spot. Rick puts the Tahoe in Drive and peels out of the parking lot.

I have done so much wrong over the last nine years; I have so much to atone for, especially with Rick, but for the life of me, I can't figure out why he is so angry with me now. I thought before we left the office that we were fine, but now he's so angry. I'm kind of afraid of him.

Before long, he heads toward our neighborhood. I wonder why we're going home when we both know Rachel isn't there. When he takes another turn and we end up in a neighborhood parallel to ours but not there yet, I wonder what he's doing.

"Rick?" I ask hesitantly as he stops for a red light.

"Hush," he responds harshly and pulls his cell phone out of his pocket and fiddles with it in his lap, popping open a little latch on the side and pulling the sim card out. He tucks the card in his breast pocket and slides another one in.

Rick unlocks the front of his screen and dials a number I'm not close enough to see as he begins driving again. I can hear a faint ring and then a terse "Hello."

"We've been compromised," Rick barks. "Time for the eagle to soar to the nest." And then he hangs up.

"Rick?"

"I need yours," he says quietly. So quietly, I almost don't hear him.

I reach in my bag and pull out my phone, handing it to him. He sets it in the cup holder between us and reaches across me to the glove box, popping it open. He pulls out a small black device that looks like an external cell phone battery and flips it on. A little green light begins blinking on top of it, and I wonder what the hell that is when he sets it under my phone in the cup holder before taking another turn, putting us on the highway.

The drive is long and silent, and the farther and farther away we get from D.C., the more worried I get. I'm sure Rick has a plan in mind, but he hasn't said one word to me about where we're going or what we're doing.

My phone beeps a weird sound I've never heard before, and Rick picks it up, punching several buttons as they pop up while he drives. It's kind of scary how he can fiddle with my phone while speeding down the interstate, but I'm too afraid to mention it. I get the feeling there is more at play than I know, and I have to wait to find out what it is, and that is not easy for me. I want to be out searching for my daughter. Someone has to have seen something.

Rick pulls off the interstate and turns down a two-lane country highway. There's nothing but farmland around for miles and miles. We stop at an old Texaco station, and Rick pays in cash before filling up. I don't even bother to unbuckle my seatbelt. I'm afraid to upset him again. I know I deserve it, but I never want to see Rick turn that kind of anger toward me again.

He climbs back in the car and buckles up before pulling out of the old gas station and continuing to drive down the highway for what seems like ages to my anxiety-ridden self. Finally, he pulls onto a long gravel drive. It winds down and around to a large farmhouse. Rick drives around the backside of the house and then to a big red barn.

Rick puts the Tahoe in Park and then reaches under his seat, pulling out a rather large-looking handgun before he climbs out. He slides open the big doors then jumps back in the car and pulls into the barn and shuts it off. I have no idea what we're doing here. I really hope this barn in the middle of nowhere isn't where I'm going to die.

He turns his body toward mine, a thunderous expression on his face. I can't help myself; I scoot backward before I can stop myself. I know that Rick would never hurt me, at least I think I do, but right now, he's just so… *terrifying*.

His face instantly blanks. It makes me wonder what's going on behind those dark eyes that seem to notice everything. I wonder what he sees when he looks at me. Can he see inside me? It scares me more than it should. I want to know what he's thinking and why he's brought me out here to this old barn.

"Cara—" he starts.

"It's okay," I interrupt him, even though we both know it's not.

"It's not." He lets out a heavy sigh. "Let's go inside."

Rick pushes open his door and steps out of the car. I unbuckle my seatbelt and follow his actions, hoping my instincts haven't led me astray. He waits for me at the back of the car, holding his hand out to me. I take it without hesitation, something that makes his face soften just a bit. I guess wondering if I trusted him or not was weighing on him more than I knew.

He leads me out of the barn before stopping to let go of my hand and pull the heavy doors closed. And then he takes my hand in his again and leads me up the back porch of the old but well-maintained house.

"Rick?" I ask.

But he holds his finger up to his lips, silencing me. "If I tell you to, you run."

I don't know what to say to that, so I just nod before he leaves me standing on the porch while he pulls the gun out of the back of his slacks, looking more than a little lethal. It's easy to see how he was such a decorated SEAL.

I wait for what seems like hours but was probably only a few minutes for him to search the house for who knows what, and I can't stand it. Finally, he puts me out of my misery, but I damn near jump out of my skin when he finally shows back up. I'm not cut out for this kind of life, and I'm from New Jersey, so that's saying something.

"It's all clear," he says, pushing open the door for me. "You can come on in now."

I nod and pass through the open door into a homey looking country kitchen. It's laid out a lot like the kitchen at my house. The house Rick bought for me. He must have some kind of thing for open concept and a lot of light, but now isn't really the time for interior design. I wonder whose house this is, not for the first time, and also what we're doing here.

"Rick?" I prompt again.

"Have a seat, Cara," he says gently, pointing to the oak table and chairs in the corner of the kitchen. I do as he asks, thinking to myself that if he wanted to kill me, there's no one here to stop him, so I might as well just get it over with.

"Where are we?" I ask quietly. It's too quiet, and we both notice the change. His face contorts back to that angry expression again.

"Jesus fuck, Cara, I'm not going to hurt you," he bites out.

"I know that," I whisper, looking away from him as he runs a frustrated hand through his hair.

"Do you?" he roars, making me flinch, which makes him even angrier. I don't understand what's going on or why he's so mad at me, all I know is that I'm scared. But I also know that Rick, no matter how mad, would never lay a hand on me.

"Yes," I say, rolling my shoulders back. I mean the words that I say to him. I think I just needed a minute to come to terms with what I already knew. Rick is upset, but he would never harm me. "I do."

"Fine," he says after a minute, when he pulls up a chair at the table.

"Where are we?" I ask again. This time, Rick turns his full attention to me, his dark eyes seeing more than I'm probably comfortable with, but this time, they don't scare me.

"My grandparents' house," he answers with the last thing I thought he would say. "They've been gone a long time. I keep the place for emergencies. No one knows it's here."

"Why are we here?" I ask, feeling more and more frustrated by the second. I hate that Rick has been badgering me for months to spill my secrets, while he ekes out information one tiny grain at a time.

"We needed a safe space to call in the cavalry," he answers. "The others will be here soon. It's time we laid it all out on the table."

"O-okay," I stammer. I think I know where this is going, and suddenly I feel really nervous. My belly flips over and over, and I'm sweaty everywhere. I think I liked it better when I thought he was going to kill me.

"Start talking," he orders.

"I was afraid you'd say that."

PRESIDENT VETOES CONTROVERSIAL BILL

CHAPTER 14

The truth revealed

"Cara," Rick growls my name, making me jump in my seat. "Now. We're running out of time."

"I don't know where to start," I admit honestly.

"The best place to start is usually the beginning." He sighs.

"All right," I tell him. "Then let's go back nine years."

"Okay," he says, his eyes snapping to meet mine, and his spine is now ramrod straight. "When? Nine years ago, be specific."

"March," I say with a sigh. "When you were deployed."

"What happened?" It's like he can barely force out the words, even though he needs to with every breath in his body. He needs to know what happened. Why our daughter was taken, why I left him with no forwarding address, why our lives derailed wholeheartedly, Rick needs to know everything. "Tell me."

"I had been feeling a little sick for a while, and finally that morning, I had my suspicions about what it was," I begin my sad tale of how we lost everything.

"Was everything all right? You're not sick now, are you?" he asks. I can hear the concern for me in his voice. Even after all this time, after everything, Rick still cares for me. It both elates me and rips open my heart.

"It was," I tell him. "I threw on a pair of running shorts and a tank and ran down to the PX on the corner. I bought the pregnancy test and then hurried home again. I didn't even read the directions. I just popped the cap, peed, and waited. I need you to know how excited I was to find out we were pregnant."

"Okay," he says without any hesitation. "I believe you. What happened next?"

"I took a shower and put on real clothes," I say, getting lost in the memory of what was the worst day of my life—that is, until today. "I grabbed my purse and jumped in the car. I headed to the Target that wasn't too far from the apartment. We needed milk and cereal. It was the only thing I could keep down in the mornings. Not to mention, I wanted that baby book everyone raves about and some prenatal vitamins. I remember thinking those vitamins were so fucking important."

"What happened next?"

"I picked up my vitamins and the book and then…" I have to pause and take a breath. It hurts so much to remember.

"And then?"

"And then I let myself walk through the baby section. I picked up the cutest pair of baby socks with little anchors on the ankles. And a baby blanket that—"

"Matches," Rick interrupts me. I can see his wheels turning. "Rachel still sleeps with it."

"She does." I smile sadly at him. "I bought them for you. I was so proud of you, and I wanted our baby to have that too, boy or girl."

"You really did tell her about me her whole life," he says like it's all suddenly clicking into place and he finally believes me at face value.

"Yes."

"Then what went so fucking wrong?" he asks as he stabs his fingers through his hair. His frustration that our lives were not ours to control is obvious. And I get it. It's a tough conclusion to come to. I've had years to adjust; Rick is just now learning about all of the dirty details.

"I went to the grocery section and picked up a big box of Cheerios. And then I headed to the dairy case. I was just reaching for a quart of milk when my phone rang. I didn't recognize the number and thought it might have been you. I was so excited to tell you about the baby. You had thought you'd be able to call that day, and you were always messing up the time difference."

"I was the worst." He laughs.

"You really were." I smile at him. "But when I answered, there were some weird pops and beeps I didn't understand. I almost hung up, but then this weird robotic voice came on. He told me that he was sending me some photos and that I needed to look at them."

"Did you?"

"Yes," I answer.

"What were they of?"

"You."

"I never cheated," he swears. "Not once."

"I know." I smile sadly. "I never doubted that. They were of you overseas. Laughing, working out, on patrol. Things like that."

"I don't understand."

"The caller told me that if I didn't leave you, you would die by friendly fire that night." I let the words hang in the air, the threat I carried with me all these years, the unspoken words of the burden I have carried that are now shared between us.

"Cara," he says gently, sadly. Rick knows and understands my sacrifice now.

"Yes." There are no other words that need to be spoken; we can't go down this road, because it won't find our daughter. We'll come back to this bridge one day, if we get our daughter back. If not… I'm not sure I'll ever go on.

"Then what happened?" he asks, and I'm thankful for the change in subject.

"I dropped the quart of milk all over the floor of Target," I admit. "The caller told me to pretend like nothing was wrong. And buy my vitamins. I decided I didn't need milk, since I would be leaving and you wouldn't be back for a long time. So I bought the things in my basket and then went back to the apartment. I left those things in the trunk of my car. I went up to the apartment and packed a bag. I didn't want to take anything else from you than I already was, so I left it all behind. Including my wedding rings.

"And then I sat on the couch as the sun set outside, and I cried and cried. I still wasn't ready when you called, but I knew what I needed to do. I had to protect you. You couldn't die because I was too selfish or too scared. So—"

"So you left me."

"I did," I answer him honestly for the first time in years. "Left as soon as I hung up the phone, driving all night. I felt restless, like I couldn't sleep. So I just kept going. And when I finally stopped at a motel to rest, I looked through a phone book, found an attorney with the least sleazy name, and asked him to file for divorce in the morning. And then I cried myself to sleep."

"And after that?"

"After that, I found a way to live without you, because I had to. I couldn't lay down and die, because we had a baby on the way, and she needed me. She still needs me."

"Cara—" he starts, but we're interrupted. I jump at the intrusion. I was so lost down our sad memory lane.

"What the fuck is going on here?" the intruder roars, making Rick roll his eyes before he turns to me.

"Cara, you know the President and First Lady of the United States."

TOP WHITE HOUSE STAFFERS NOTICEABLY ABSENT IN D.C.

CHAPTER 15

"Cara!" Grace says, rushing toward me. My spine stiffens. I'm not sure what's going to happen next, and then she envelops me in a fierce hug. "I was so worried!"

"It's okay," I say softly.

"It's not okay!" she's still yelling. One thing I've noticed about Grace is that the normally cool, calm, and collected former attorney is kind of a livewire now that pregnancy hormones are coursing through her body.

"Let's all move this into the living room," Rick suggests. "Then we can brief you guys on the situation."

Jake lets out a frustrated sigh. "We might as well wait. Ryan is bringing Jules. As much as I want all the info right now, you should wait to brief us all at once."

"Is it a good idea to bring Black into the fold?" Rick asks, and I wonder what the fuck they're talking about.

"It is," Jake says. "You can trust him."

Rick clenches his jaw and then releases it. "Fine."

"I know you don't like him—" Jake starts.

"I don't know him," Rick interrupts. "He's too private."

We all file into the living room and take our seats. Jake pulls Grace in to share an oversized armchair with him, and I look away. My cheeks heat at their public display. They may have started as enemy sharks swimming in the same big, New York pond, but now they are the real deal. I love Grace, and I'm so happy she's found her forever. And so very sorry I played a part in hurting her before they figured it all out. She's long since forgiven me, but I haven't. Not yet.

Gus, Jake's main Secret Service agent, and Joe, his driver plus, file in and flank the room, always at the ready. It must be hard not having any privacy at all. Although it doesn't seem to bother Jake and Grace much. Rick, for the most part, has always been on the fringes and out of the limelight. I wonder how he straddles the line.

I'm distracted by my thoughts when Jules barrels into the room spitting mad, with the president's aide-de-camp hot on her heels.

"Would you kindly get your paws off me!" she snaps before coming to a halt as she notices the full room. "What's going on here?"

"Sit down, Jules," Jake says quietly. "This is serious."

"What's happened?" she asks, her demeanor instantly changing from pissed off lioness to alert as she drops to the arm of the sofa farthest away from me. I notice the captain stands with his back against the wall. His limbs hang loose, giving the impression he is relaxed, but the marine is anything but.

"Rachel has been taken," Rick says to the room.

Jake closes his eyes for a second before opening them again, and when he does, they burn bright with determination and retribution.

"Is there any connection between her kidnapping and this morning's revelations?" Jake asks.

"I think so," Rick says.

"Is this place even secure?" Captain Black bites out.

"Yes," Jake replies calmly, his voice even when I can tell he feels anything but. "This property is secure and off public records. Rick and I meet here often."

The captain nods once before yielding the floor. "All right."

"What makes you think the two events are connected?" Jake asks.

Rick wraps his arm around my shoulders from

where he sits on the arm of the sofa next to me. He squeezes my shoulder once, a signal to be brave and hang tight while we get through all this, and then he lets go before answering his best friend and boss.

"Nine years ago, Cara and I were married," Rick says to those in the room who did not know. Grace and Jake's faces are both carefully blank.

"What?" Jules asks.

"And nine years ago, Cara left me when Jake and I were deployed."

Captain Black's eyes narrow on me for a split second. His judgment is evident and finding me lacking.

"Ouch," Grace whispers.

"She was blackmailed," Rick adds.

"What?" Jake barks out.

"I was sent pictures of Rick overseas and told that if I didn't leave him, he would die by friendly fire that night," I answer them.

"So you left," Jake adds.

"Yes."

"To protect Donovan," Black adds as he openly appraises me, only this time I don't feel like he finds I come up short. I don't know why his approval matters; it just does.

"Yes," I answer him, meeting his gaze and showing him that I'm neither lying nor afraid. He accepts my answer with a nod.

"When was this?" Jake asks.

"March," Rick and I reply at the same time.

"About when we were assigned to cartel op?" Jake asks with a raised brow.

"The one and the same," Rick growls.

"Well," Jake says, steepling his fingers together and reminding me of the little poem Rachel would re-cite when she was a toddler as she folded her chubby fingers the same way. "That is interesting."

"That's what I thought," Rick states casually, making Captain Black lose his patience.

"Care to share with the fucking class?" Black barks.

"Yes," Jake says, clearly enjoying riling up his aide. "As you know, Rick and I were on the same SEAL team. On one deployment, we were presented with an off-the-books mission. It seemed… off. But we were young and dumb and weren't necessarily in the market to question orders that came from way above our pay grade."

"Or we would have, if I hadn't been on a one-man suicide mission," Rick adds, making me gasp.

"No," I say before I can stop myself.

Rick gives me a sad smile. "I was pretty messed up after my wife left me," he says. "I jumped at any mission they gave me. It didn't matter how dangerous. And if it seemed like a one-way ticket, even better."

"Rick—"

"And I was there for my brother," Jakes says. "And

I had no intention of running for office when my dad retired."

"But this one was different," Rick finishes.

"Different, how?" Black asks.

"It didn't go as planned and people died," Rick admits.

"And you think this mission is connected?" he asks the two of them.

"Yes," they both say in unison.

"Why?"

"Because of what the blackmailers mentioned," Jake replies.

"They said, 'Old ghosts will rise, and others will pay the price. Pass the bill or pay the price,'" Black recites.

"No," Rick corrects. "It said the 'Old Ghost' as in singular and—"

"My old callsign," Jake inserts.

"Someone knows way more than they should," Rick says, sending chills down my spine.

"Who else would know about that op?" Captain Black asks.

"We should call Wes and Lee," Rick says from beside me.

"Just to warn them, but that op was after they got out," Jake agrees with him.

"I'll call now and put it on speakerphone," Rick

suggests, and Jake nods in agreement.

Rick slips his phone out of his pocket, the one with the new sim card, and swipes his finger across the glass to unlock it when he types in his code. He selects the phone app and dials in a number by heart before pressing the speakerphone button. The ringing sound fills the room, and we all collectively hold our breath.

"Special Agent O'Connell," a deep voice answers. Wes was one of the few friends I met when Rick and I were dating. It was only once in a bar in San Diego, but he was kind and welcoming, even if there was an almost sad aura around him.

"It's Donovan," Rick says.

"And Chancey," Jake says.

"Well why wasn't I invited to the party?" Wes laughs.

"It's not so much a party," Rick says darkly. "But we'll get to that in a minute."

"You wouldn't be near Goodie's office, would you?" Jake asks, always the diplomatic one. Rick used to be just as charismatic and yielding. Is this what I did to him? Did I make him this brute of a man? Something tells me I better be prepared for the answer when it comes, because it won't be a sweet and gentle fairy tale.

"No," Wes answers. "With Claire on desk duty now that she's as big as a house, and if you repeat that, I will not only deny ever having said it, but I will help her hide your miserable fucking bodies."

"So pregnancy agrees with your blushing bride?" Jake laughs, which is ironic, because Grace is just as terrifying. She looks at me, and I can tell she knows what I'm thinking, because she raises a delicately sculpted brow—the one she cussed me out over while I waxed them—at me in challenge. I just stick my tongue out at her and shrug, making her laugh.

"No fucking way," Wes grumbles. "I love her, but she's a monster."

"That sounds like how Angie was." Jules laughs.

"I was just thinking the same," Grace agrees with her on the antics of their college friend I've only ever heard about secondhand. She was at the inauguration; I just didn't have time to meet her, because the newly minted Chief of Staff was dragging me from the building to have his wicked way with me.

"So Goodie isn't around?" Jake asks, bringing the conversation back around.

"No," Wes says, and I can hear his heavy sigh across the line. "With Claire on desk duty and miserable, he's having to cover her field work. There's something heating up in the area that sounds like it might be ready to shift to my office, but I'm actually out of town at the moment working another case. I'll be happy to pass the word on though."

"Something has come up here, and it looks like it's linked to a mission we carried out after you guys got out, but I just wanted to give you the heads up," Jake tells him.

"Funny you should mention that," Wes says, not sounding like anything is funny at all. "The case I'm working on?"

"Yeah?" Rick says.

"I'm in Virginia. Palmer is dead."

"What?" Rick asks.

"When?" Jake questions.

"It's recent," Wes answers. "He ate a bullet."

"Fuck," Rick bites out. "I didn't know he was struggling."

"No one did," Wes replies. "I had just seen him at Claire's shower. He seemed fine."

"I'm sorry," Rick says. "So fucking sorry."

"Me too." Wes sighs. "Anyways, it sounds like there's more to your story than 'some shit came up over an old mission.'"

"You'd be right," Rick says, closing his eyes tight. "Someone kidnapped my daughter after blackmailing my wife."

"I'll be at your house in D.C. at nine," he states and then hangs up.

"Typical Wes," Rick grumbles, making Jake laugh. "Still calling orders."

"Looks like the gang is getting back together."

"So what now?" Captain Black asks.

"I think we need to figure out who could be behind this," Jake responds.

"And we need a plan to get my daughter back," Rick growls.

"Oo-rah!" Gus, Joe, and Captain Black all shout.

"I can't help but feel like this all goes back to getting to the president," Captain Black says. "I don't know the story as well as you do, but—"

"But what?" Rick asks.

"It all sounds to me like someone is moving the pieces on a chessboard, and it all goes back to the president. I think we need to go way back before they were married. Before Mrs. Donovan was even in the picture."

"We're going to need sustenance for that," Jules says. "Is there any food in this joint?

"The freezer and pantry should be fully stocked," Rick says. "I don't come out here enough to keep perishables in the fridge."

"Excellent," she says as she claps her hands and jumps up to move into action. Grace tries to jump up too, but her heavy belly has her off balance and a little stuck.

"Fuck," she bites out. "Jules, give me a hand or I'll never get up."

"Well, why didn't you say something, darling?" Jake's eyes twinkle before he lifts her up like she weighs nothing at all and sets her on her feet. "There you go."

"Yes, thank you," she says, making it sound like a

blatant threat. Jake pats her on her backside, making her growl before she stomps off into the kitchen behind Jules.

"Uhh… I should go make sure she doesn't poison the president," I say, making the room chuckle to various degrees.

Rick just smiles at me. "I think they'll be fine," he says to me before placing a gentle kiss on my temple.

"Now, where were we?" Captain Black asks.

WHISPERS OF COLLUSION SMACK WHITE HOUSE

CHAPTER 16

Power doesn't come cheap

"I'll… uhh… just go see to that coffee," I say as I stand up to scurry out of the room. The sound of masculine chuckles following behind me.

"She's not used to so much talk of missions and political intrigue," I hear Rick say quietly as I walk away.

"How much did you share with her when you were married?" Captain Black asks.

"Nothing."

"Ouch," he replies to Rick.

"I'm regretting that now."

"She saved your life," I hear him whisper just as I slip into the kitchen, but it's Rick's words that ring in my ears and play over and over in my head, and probably will for the rest of my life.

"I know."

"Cara?" I look up when I hear Jules calling my name. "Honey, are you okay?"

"I don't know," I say honestly. "They're kind of scary out there."

She gives me a knowing smile that I wonder more about. "I think with you they're more bark than bite."

"What about with you?" I ask and immediately wish I could call the words back into my mouth.

"What about me?" She laughs, but it doesn't seem all too genuine. "I can run with the big boys. I don't need to be cared for."

Something about her words makes Grace stop her freezer raid of frozen pizzas and shoots Jules a weird look. I wonder what's going on there. I look to Grace, and she shakes her head quickly before Jules can see our exchange.

"I came to help with… whatever it is that's going on in here," I say, making both women laugh. "What am I missing?"

"We were gossiping," Grace admits.

"I don't doubt it," I add. "Why leave me out? That's not fair!"

"We were talking *about* you," she admits.

"Well, thanks for that."

"It was all good," Grace says quickly.

"It was brave what you did," Jules adds softly. Her

tone surprises me, making my eyes snap back to her. She really means that.

"Or stupid," I admit what's been bothering me the most. "I feel like I've done nothing but play into their hands. Whoever they are."

I walk over to the coffeemaker; it's an old Mr. Coffee, and the sight of it makes me smile. I needed this bit of real life in the midst of these powerful people and their fancy shit. I'm more of the blue-collar hanger-on they like for some reason, and I'm not even sure about that. It's probably Rachel. Everyone loves her.

I feel a sob bubble up in my chest, and I choke it back while I pour water into the coffeemaker. This is so fucking unfair. I layer a paper filter into the bowl and scoop coffee grounds into it. Rachel loves to paint filters like this one with watercolors and make sun catchers. I have to grip the counter tight at the memory as it hits me like a fist to the belly. How could I have been so stupid? I knew they would make good on their threats, and I took one more night with Rick anyway. He's my weakness, and he always has been.

But now it's going to cost me my only child.

I don't even think about what I'm doing as I grab the bag of coffee grounds, hurl them across the kitchen, and scream. I scream with everything I have, because this is all so unfair. I scream and scream, because there's nothing else I can do.

"Jake!" I hear Grace shout, but I don't care. I'm too lost in my grief.

I drop to my knees and slam my palms against the floor. The coffee grounds grate against my skin. She can't be gone! I can't live without her. I lay my forehead down on the old linoleum floor, and tears course down my face. Through it all, I keep screaming. My voice is harsh to my own ears; its rasp is painful to hear.

"Ryan! Rick!" Jules shouts. "Come quick!"

I hear heavy footfalls, and still I don't care. How could I care about anything right now? Or ever again? Nothing matters now. All that matters is Rachel.

Strong arms close around me and hold me tight. I struggle. I don't want this. I don't want to be calm. I want to fight.

"Hush," Rick says calmly as he pulls me into his lap, but it only serves to make me struggle more.

"No!" I scream. In my frantic attempt at flight, I see everyone file out of the kitchen quietly, but I don't care. "Let me go."

"No."

"Let me go!" I scream.

"Never!" Rick roars back. He holds me tighter.

"You have to let me go," I cry harder. "This is all my fault."

"It's not."

"It is!" I sob as Rick cradles me in his arms. "I could have stopped this."

"No, honey," he says sadly. "They always would

have come for me."

"Why Rachel?" I rasp, my voice is now completely shattered. "Why my baby?"

"I'm going to get her back," Rick promises as he tucks my face into the crook of his neck. "You have to believe me. I'm going to get her back."

"It should have been me," I pant as my chest feels too tight. I can't get a breath in. I claw at my neck, but it's no use.

As it turns out, those were the last words I spoke before everything went black.

Apparently, now is the time to panic.

WHITE HOUSE
CHIEF OF STAFF
MOVES EX INTO
HIS HOUSE.
HEARTS
AFLUTTER

CHAPTER 17

Settle in

"Hello?" I hear Rick's deep voice answer his phone after it rings somewhere deeper in the house, and I open my eyes.

I feel like shit.

My throat is rough and scratchy, and my head is pounding. Thick crust coats my eyelashes, and after the epic meltdown I had, I'm guessing I look like a cousin of Quasimodo.

I look around. I'm lying in a rough pine log bed that's probably barely a double bed. Matching furniture is scattered all around the room, and bare light-yellow walls that have aged with time, but were obviously still cared for, surround us. On a better day, I would wonder how often Rick finds time to come out here and remember his grandparents, people I had never gotten the chance to meet.

"Hey, baby," he says as he sits down in the crook of my legs, his phone call clearly over.

"Hi," I say, brushing my hair back from my face. Someone must have taken down my bun.

"How are you feeling?" Rick smooths the palm of his hand up and down the outside of my thigh. It's not sexual; it's comforting, almost like he's gentling a spooked horse.

"Like hammered horse shit," I respond, making him smile enough that the sides of his eyes crinkle. The Rick of my youth didn't have as many lines around his eyes where now they're more prominent, but this Rick is older, more seasoned, and no less handsome. If anything, age has made him better-looking.

"What are you thinking about?" he asks softly.

"That you got better-looking with age, and I just got old." I laugh, but the laughter dies in my throat when his palm lands flat on the outside of my ass. The crack was just enough to sting.

"Ouch, what was that for?" I ask as I rub the skin to soothe the burn.

"You are not old," he says while making an angry face. "And I'm still older."

"Yeah, but you're hot and still in great shape," I admit before patting my tummy. "And I got squishy."

"I had no life outside of work before you came back," he growls. "And I like you soft."

"Thanks," I respond, rolling my eyes.

"If we were alone, I'd show you how much I like it, but I think you already know."

The reminder of where we are and why shoots ice water through my veins, cooling my pique. "Yeah."

"Hey," he says. "It's going to be okay."

"How can you say that?" I demand, pushing up from the bed and away from Rick. "Don't make promises you can't keep."

"Like you," he strikes with his words, ripping my heart in two. "I seem to remember you promising forever and then running at the first hurdle."

"That's not fair."

"You know what's not fair?" he asks me but doesn't give me a chance to answer, which is probably a good thing, seeing as the list of my transgressions grows by the minute. "That I was denied a life with you and our daughter, and now that it's all out on the table, you're still running."

"I'm not running."

"Good," his voice rumbles in his chest. "Because I think I've made myself perfectly clear."

"Oh yeah?" I snap. "How's that?"

"If you run, I'll chase you. Simple as that."

Simple as that.

But it's not. Nothing is simple at all. Rick is lying to himself and me if he thinks this can end well at all. I know he's just telling me what I want to hear, but I'm tired of lying and being lied to. Why can't we just be honest with each other? Why does it always have to be so damn complicated between Rick and me? I can't keep doing this. I said my goodbyes already, so if Rick wants to keep pretending everything will work out all right in the end, that's fine by me, but I won't be here to play his games.

"I need to get back home," I say as I push to sit up.

"So that's how we're going to play it?" he asks, eyeing me speculatively.

"Play what, Rick?" I push out a frustrated breath. "I'm not playing at anything."

"Sure," he murmurs. "We can go back home."

"Thank you," I say, letting out the breath I hadn't known I'd been holding. It's a huge relief, if I'm being honest. I was afraid Rick wasn't going to let me go back to my life, not that I could go back to things the way they were after everything that happened, but I needed space to figure out what I could do to help my daughter. Maybe I could call the kidnappers back and offer a trade, her for me. But I can't let Rick know that's the plan, so getting some much-needed space to figure things out and get my head on straight is a huge boon.

And if life taught me anything so far, it's not to count my chickens before they hatch. Not that I had seen many chickens in a group foster home near Newark, but still, I heard the saying many times, and still, I didn't heed the warning. Clearly, I should have, because the expression on Rick's rugged face can only be described as irritated, so when he opens his mouth to respond, I should have known I wasn't getting my prayers answered—not today, not any day.

"Not so fast," he grumbles.

"What?" I ask, knowing I shouldn't have opened my mouth, but I did anyway.

"You're not going back to your house."

"What? Why not?"

"Because you're coming home with me," he says, and there's a finality to his words that shuts down every rebuttal I could have conceived. "Get ready to leave."

And then he stands up and leaves me in the bedroom to straighten my appearance before we leave his family home. If I had something worthy of throwing nearby, I might have been tempted. Instead, I let out a frustrated growl low enough he shouldn't have been able to hear it. Of course, he does anyway, because that is my life.

"Go ahead and let that Jersey Girl temper out," he shouts from the other room. "Nothing makes my cock harder faster than you in a temper tantrum."

"It's not a temper tantrum, you ass!" I shout back before I can stop myself.

"Still hard though." He chuckles. "I've got a great way for you to work out all that aggression, baby."

"Shut. Up."

"I'm ready when you are," he says, letting the double meaning of his words hang in the air.

"Well go on and keep waiting," I grumble as I push up from the bed.

I quickly fold the covers back to where they were. Even as irritated with him as I am, I can't leave Rick's family home in shambles. I find my shoes in the process and slide my feet into them before shutting off the light and walking out the bedroom door.

Rick is waiting for me in the living room. I expected him to be smug about his ability to get under my skin, but he is nothing but the picture of patience, like some kind of ninja warrior ready to wait me out and goddammit, why can't he ever be as off-balance as I always seem to be? It's so unfair.

"I'm ready," I say, sounding more than a little irritated, and I swear I see a twitch in the corner of his mouth like he wants to smile but knows he shouldn't, because I am clearly a woman on the edge.

"Perfect. After you," he says before holding the door open for me to pass through into the kitchen.

I follow him out onto the porch and watch as he locks up the house. When he's finished his task, we walk out into the side yard and to the old barn where he stored the car. Rick slides the heavy panel door back, and we head inside.

He beeps the locks on his SUV, and we climb inside. I buckle my seatbelt silently as he starts the car. I can see out of my peripheral vision that he turns to me like he wants to say something, but I don't give him my attention. Instead, I keep my gaze focused out the dark windshield. Rick seems to get the cold-shoulder message I'm sending and shakes his head before throwing the car in Reverse and backing out of the old barn.

He puts the car in Park and jumps out, running back to the door of the barn and slides it closed before locking it up tight. When he's done, Rick runs back to the SUV and jumps in the driver seat, shutting his door behind him. He buckles his seatbelt and then we're off into the night.

We don't talk; in fact, I don't utter a single word over the course of our long drive back to the city. Instead, I plot and plan. I have to get away from Rick. His presence is suffocating me slowly while I'm dying to try to find a way to save my daughter. It was my fault, my doing that put her in danger, and I'm going to get her out of it.

He hits the clicker for his garage door, and the heavy metal panels slide up, giving entrance to his fortress. He drives inside and cuts the engine before hitting the button again to lower the door, sealing us in.

Rick unbuckles his seatbelt and pushes his door open, stepping down. He doesn't come around to open my door or offer me a hand. Instead, he stands there, patiently waiting for me to follow him inside his house while my own home sits mere feet away.

"I'm going to need things from my house," I tell him, an idea popping into my head as a plan begins to form. "It would be so much easier for me to stay there."

"Don't even think about it," he warns, his voice low and commanding, and I do not like it at all.

"Rick—" I start.

"Absolutely not."

"You're not the boss of me!" I stomp my foot.

"You like it when I'm bossy," he responds, crowding me in. My back hits the wall behind me, and my skin flushes. How he always manages to make my own body betray me, I will never know. "I seem to recall you enjoying just how… *bossy* I can get the other night."

"My things?" I ask and my voice sounds high pitched and thready.

"Sure," Rick agrees with a stupid smirk on his face. "I'll make sure to get your things."

"Thank you."

"After I see that you're settled in."

"Fine." We could play it his way, as Rick suggested earlier. I could stay in his house, and he could fetch my belongings when he decides I can have them, but at the first available opportunity, I'm going to run again, because nothing is going to get between me and my daughter, not even an overprotective man who thinks he knows best. And one thing is certain. I'm not going to settle in, not now, not ever.

CRITICS WANT TO KNOW: WHAT DOES THE PRESIDENT HAVE AGAINST NEW BILL?

CHAPTER 18

One World Nation

The doorbell rings, surprising me.

"Who is that?"

"That would be Wes," Rick answers me as he makes his way to the front door. Everything about his manner speaks of a casual, easygoing man, but there's a way he reaches for the gun tucked into the back of his jeans that says otherwise. There is so much more to this man than I ever knew. It makes him dangerous. Dangerous to me, to my heart, and to my panties.

Immediately after declaring I was not going home, Rick steered me—like a border collie would his flock of sheep—up the stairs and toward his bedroom, making me on edge. I might not know Rick very well anymore, but even I was pretty sure he thought finding our daughter was more important that fucking around, literally.

"Relax," he whispered gruffly in my ear. "If I was intending to fuck you right now, you'd know it."

"You can stop talking any time now," I replied as he started opening drawers and pulling an array of clothes out.

"Why?" he asked as he shucked his suit coat from his body, dropping it on a chair in the corner of his room before reaching for the knot of his tie, loosening it to pull it over his head. "This is so much fun."

I watched with rapt attention, my mouth going dry as he neatly plucked at the row of buttons down the front of his dress shirt one by one. I should be used to seeing his strong shoulders and muscular arms by now. I shouldn't have trouble schooling my thoughts at the sight of his chiseled abs, and yet I do. And by the knowing look on his stupidly handsome face, Rick knows it too.

He takes the gun from the back of his slacks and places it within reach on top of the tall five-drawer dresser where he was pulling clothes from. It was a stark reminder that our lives were not all fun and games right now. How he could find it in him to joke or to flirt at a time like this, I don't think I will ever understand.

"You have to find light moments in the dark or else you'll break, Cara," he told me with a heavy sigh. "I'm afraid that when you finally break, it'll be for good, and I won't ever be able to get you back."

"I don't need to find light in the dark. I need to find

my daughter."

"As do I," he warned me, his voice no longer friendly as he stripped off his slacks and yanked a worn pair of Levi's up his legs, buttoning the fly as quickly as possible. "Don't you dare accuse me of not trying."

"I'm not," I said quickly as he stabbed his arms through a light gray T-shirt that fit him like a second skin and pulled it down over his head. "I don't know what I'm doing. But… it feels wrong to joke, to flirt, to—"

"Fuck?" he filled in for me.

"Yes," I grumble.

"In my line of work, you learn that life is short and can be taken from you in a split second," he said, snapping his fingers.

"Don't say that."

"It's true, honey," he said, stepping into me and pulling me into his arms. He brushed the hair back from my face but held my head so I had to look him in the eyes. "I'm serious, and I'm also trying to be gentle with you. But you need to learn to take life as it comes. You can't let that darkness and the fear keep you from living, because it's the only life you'll ever get."

"I'm not—" I started to say, but he silenced me with a kiss. It wasn't passionate, and he didn't get carried away. It was just a press of his lips against mine to stop the flow of words from my mouth.

"You are," he said before pressing his lips to mine

again then taking them away all too soon. "I lived my life without you for nine years, and honey, I'm not going to do it again. And in those nine years, I've not only seen so much darkness, but I lived it, I thrived in it, and I absorbed it into my soul. So now that I've had a taste of your sweetness and your fire and your light again, I know how much I need it like I need my next breath. So I'm going to find reasons to rile you up, and I'm going to make up excuses to kiss you, and I'm not going to need one excuse to fuck you, because I need you like I need air. But mark my words—I am going to find our daughter, and I need you to trust me to do that too."

"Okay," I whispered, because I didn't know what else to say.

He let go of me to reach back over to the dresser, where he grabbed one of his T-shirts, a pair of navy-blue sweats that read NAVY up the leg in yellow block letters, and a pair of thick, wooly socks. He stacked them in a bundle and handed them to me with a kiss to my temple.

"Get comfortable and meet me downstairs," he said before checking the magazine in the gun and then tucking it into the back of his jeans, sauntering out of the room like he hadn't just tipped my entire universe on its head.

So I quickly stripped off my summer dress and pulled on his clothes, taking a moment to sniff them, because they smelled like him, and I had almost let myself forget just how much I missed his scent. How much I missed the very man himself.

And then I walked downstairs to find out what else he had in store for me. I was just about to open my mouth to ask him, when the doorbell rang.

"Who is that?"

"That would be Wes," Rick answers me. He looks through the window to the left of the door before pulling it open with a huge smile on his face. "Good to see you, brother."

"It's been too long," the man, just as giant as Rick, says when he makes his way into the house, and I recognize him instantly. Wes O'Connell hasn't changed much. He still has dark hair and hazel eyes, a lot like Rick, but where Wes has angular, classically handsome features, Rick looks rougher, darker, hotter. Wes is good-looking, but Rick inspires my fantasies. He always has and probably always will.

"Hi." I wave nervously when the semi-famous FBI agent turns his attention to me.

"Hi." He smiles gently at me, and it transforms his whole face. Then he turns to Rick and says, "I see what you mean."

"Yeah." Rick smiles a funny smile that makes my belly go all wobbly.

"She's pretty," Wes says. "Seriously pretty. But it's the whole awkward and uncomfortable but she'll make the best out of it vibe that knocks it out of the park."

"Yeah," Rick agrees while they continue talking about me like I'm not even here. "And she's got a great ass."

"Hey!" I shout. "I'm right here."

"I know," Rick says, wrapping his arms around me.

"Ugh. What do you want?" I roll my eyes. They are both ridiculous, and my nerves are too frayed to deal with them right now. At another time, I would love to hear all about how Wes went back and got the girl after all, and how they became semi-famous back in Jersey. How funny that we're from the same state, but I grew up not far from the shore, and they grew up in North Jersey. It's a small world after all.

"You," Rick says without missing a beat.

"I hate to interrupt…" Wes leads in.

"No, you don't," Rick replies to his friend with a smile on his face.

"That's true," Wes admits as he starts hunting for the kitchen. "Got any beer or a decent pizza place around here?"

"Yes on the beer," Rick calls out.

"Don't hold your breath on the pizza," I answer. "But it's passable."

"Ugh," Wes groans. "I miss home."

"I just miss the pizza." And my daughter, but I didn't want to be a Debbie Downer when these two hadn't seen each other in a while. Plus, we need to find out what everyone knows, so we can piece it all to-gether.

"I'll order some," Rick says, pulling his phone from his pocket.

I make my way into the kitchen, find a glass, and fill it with tap water. I gulp the contents of the glass down before filling it up again.

"Thirsty?" Wes asks from behind me. I feel my spine stiffen and a startled gasp catch in my throat. Truthfully, I had forgotten he was there for a minute, so he had surprised me. I wasn't cut out for this cloak-and-dagger life.

"I'm… uhh… fine," I answer. My voice sounds gruff to my own ears, but hopefully Wes doesn't notice.

He looks toward the living room where we can hear Rick on the phone with the pizza place. Wes is clearly weighing his words and deciding how much time he has to threaten me if I break his buddy's heart again. I literally don't have time for such trivial conversations. I can't stand all this waiting around. I need to do something.

I'm about to make some flippant comment to Wes when he turns his attention back to me. His hazel eyes burn bright at me, and for a second, it feels like he sees all my secrets. I wonder what kind of voodoo magic they train them in at the FBI.

"He's not a bad guy, you know," Wes says quietly, my guess so that Rick won't hear.

"I never said he was."

"But you still won't give him a chance?" he asks me, and the look he gives me could be described as no less than disappointed.

"We never had a chance." I sigh.

"No offense, but that's bullshit," Wes clips.

"In my experience, when someone starts off with 'no offense,' it means that's exactly what they are about to do, so why don't you save your bullshit judgment for someone else," I bite out.

"No," he says, folding his arms across his chest. The move is infuriating. How dare he judge me and my life, when he's met me a grand total of three times in my entire life. Fuck him.

"No?" He did not just say no to me when I told him to let it the fuck go. I've been feeling like I'm chaffing against the world all day. Like I can't get comfortable, because I'm the puzzle piece that doesn't fit, and it has rubbed me raw all day. I'm spoiling for a fight, and if Wes really wants one, I'll be happy to oblige him.

"That's what I said, no."

"You are more of a bitter bag of dicks than I remembered, Wes, so why don't you do us both a favor and butt out."

"I could say the same about you, darlin'," he snarls on a saccharine-sweet smile.

"Do not start with me," I warn. "You don't know anything about me."

"I know you're a coward," he says calmly. "And I know that man in there would kiss the ground you walk on if you let him. I know he would offer you the moon if it would make you happy, let alone a beautiful life if you let him, but you're so caught up in your own miserable bullshit that you won't ever give him a chance."

"What chance?" I practically shout. "We had a chance nine years ago, and I gave it all up, *for him*, so don't you stand there and look down your nose at me."

"And it's within your grasp again, and what are you doing?" he asks, looking at me like I'm nothing but a dog turd on his shoe. "You're running. I see it. You're just waiting for an opportunity to run again."

"I have to find my daughter!" I grip my hair in my hands, pulling it roughly from its messy bun.

"You don't think he feels the same way?" Wes snarls at me. "You don't think he's dying inside? He finally found the family he thought slipped through his fingers nine years ago, and he is feeling her absence greatly, but you're still only thinking about you. What about him?"

And then after he finishes tossing my world on its head, he tosses back the rest of his beer before dropping the glass bottle in the trashcan and stalking from the room without offering me so much as a backward glance or a "See you on the flipside."

And to be honest, I don't really blame him. After what he said, I can't help but feel like a monster. Have I been so caught up in my own head that I haven't bothered to think of Rick? It kind of lessons the sacrifices I made for him years ago. Maybe I'm as bad as Wes thinks.

I fill up my glass one more time before grabbing two more beers from the fridge and carrying them all into the dining room that sits between the living room and kitchen. I set my water on the table and carry the beers to where the guys are talking in low tones so I won't hear them. We watch each other warily as I approach them.

"Another beer?" I ask as I hold them out in front of me.

"Thanks," Wes says as he eyes the still capped bottle cautiously. I wanted him to realize I didn't spit in it when I could have.

"Thanks, baby," Rick says softly before taking the bottle from me.

"Sure." I try to step back, feeling really unwelcome in this little powwow, when Rick pulls me into his side and holds me tight. Ever since this morning, he's been finding ways to keep me close to him, to hold me or touch me in some sweet way or another. I don't even know if he realizes he's doing it, but all of a sudden, he's always in contact with me physically if he can be.

A knock sounds at the door.

"That would probably be the pizza," Rick says, letting me go.

Wes tenses as he watches Rick approach the front door. I see them both hold their bodies loose, like they're ready to spring into action, but you wouldn't know it's coming unless you know what you're looking for.

Rick looks casually out the side window just as he did when Wes showed up and decides it's safe. Pulling open the door, Rick hands the kid a couple twenties and tells him to keep the change before accepting the stack of pizza boxes and shutting the door behind him, throwing the lock closed.

He carries the pizza boxes into the dining room and sets them on the table. Wes and I follow behind him. When I get there, I realize I forgot plates and napkins, so I scurry back into the kitchen to grab them. Wes's words about how I could do a better job looking after Rick are still weighing heavy on my brain. He's right. I haven't been looking after the man I swore up and down I loved no matter what, when I should have. Instead, I only thought about me and how it made me feel.

I set a stack of plates and napkins down on the table and take a seat. Wes and Rick waited for me to return to the table before sitting down. He might hate me, or at least he used to, now I'm not so sure. I'm not sure where we stand at all, and I've done so much wrong, but he has manners, and that is an interesting combination.

I pass plates around while the guys lift lids on different pizzas and start passing the boxes around the table. Rick puts three slices of pepperoni and anchovy on my plate. It's my favorite and he knows it. I didn't have to ask; he just provided a comfort staple for me. I have to swallow back against the lump in my throat.

"Thanks," I say softly.

"Of course."

I pick at my plate. I really am the worst. I need to put forth more of an effort to make sure he's okay. But overall, I'm miserable. It's never a fun moment having your worst failings thrown in your face—whether or not you deserve them. When Rick notices that my glass is almost empty, he stands up and heads to the kitchen. Wes shoots me a pointed stare.

"I know," I say sadly. "You were right. I'm a monster."

"You're not a monster," he replies, rolling his eyes. "You can fix it."

"But how?" I ask as I pluck a piece of anchovy and pop it in my mouth. "I've been so awful."

"You know that's disgusting, right?"

"Don't knock it until you try it." I smile just a little bit. "Rick hates it too, but he still buys it for me."

"Because he's in love with you."

"What makes you think so?" I ask, popping another bite into my mouth. I have loved Rick and lived without him for so long, I've done so everything the wrong way, and still I hope that after all of it, he can find it in his heart to forgive me and love me the way that I love him. But I'm still terrified that he won't be able to let it all go.

"I know the look of a man chasing a woman so desperately he doesn't know what to do with himself," he says on a smirk. "And I know the look of a woman running more from what's in her own damn head than anything else."

"She's a lucky woman," I say softly.

"And after a fair amount of time, she knows it now," he says, and a happy look of a man content with his life washes over him. I'm glad he has that. He's not a bad guy. I shouldn't wish him ill.

Just then, Rick comes back into the room, and I wonder if he was listening at the door like a teenage girl. He sets down a glass of water in front of me and another beer for each of them.

"So are you done listening in like a little bitch?" Wes asks on a laugh, making Rick scowl.

"I'm not a little bitch."

"But you were listening in?" I ask.

"Maybe," he admits, eyeing me speculatively.

"Care to add anything?" Wes prompts with a twinkle in his eye.

"No, I think you covered all of the basics," Rick says while rolling his eyes. "Now, let's figure out who's so desperate to blackmail the president that they would kidnap my daughter."

Finally. Now we're getting somewhere.

Wes pulls a notepad and pen out of his jeans pocket, and Rick drops a legal pad on the table. He spins a pen in his hand like a majorette with a marching band. I hold my breath. There has to be something between the two of them that leads us to Rachel.

"So what do you have?" Wes asks.

"This morning, Cara received a video message from the kidnappers…" Rick explains to Wes how we broke up nine years ago and why.

"So why do you think they targeted you two if the goal was always Jake?" Wes asks.

"I never would have taken those suicide missions and off-books ops if it weren't for my divorce," Rick explains, making me cringe. I hate that I changed him so much, but it also changed me, and I can't lose sight of that. We're not who we used to be. "Cara kept me grounded, and without her, I was adrift. I didn't care what the mission was as long as it took me away from home where I would sit and think about why she left me. Removing her from the game made me that mercenary."

And Jake would never let you go into a shit situation half-cocked," Wes adds. "They knew he would go with you."

"And when we both couldn't take it anymore, we got out, and he eventually got talked into running for office."

"Who talked him into it?" Wes asks.

"Mostly, he was worn down by his dad, the senior senator," Rick says.

"I bet he's over the moon that Jake won the presidency," Wes inserts.

"Yes and no," Rick answers. "Jake made it clear

that his dad's shady dealings would not have sway over Jake."

"I bet the old man loved that." Wes whistles.

"He did not. And Jake won't let him near Grace either."

"So could it be him?" I ask, not censoring my words at all. "Sorry, I shouldn't have interrupted."

"It could be, but I doubt it," Rick says gently. "It seems a little too obvious."

"You're right," I reply quietly. Embarrassment burns my cheeks.

"Hey," he says softly, drawing my attention. "It's not wrong to ask."

"Okay."

"Someone wants this bill to pass badly," Rick points out. "It's the only thing I can think of."

"What bill?" Wes asks.

"Specifically, HB 2250," Rick answers. "It's the 'Spread the Wealth' bill."

"The one that would send US money and weapons overseas?" Wes asks.

"The one and only," Rick answers, and I think I should start paying more attention to the news. "Not only that, but it places huge limitations on the US government and what we're allowed to do to protect ourselves and our people. Essentially, it ties the hands of the US military."

"But why would anyone want that?" I ask, feeling stupid. Why don't I know these things? I feel like I should know these things.

"Power," Rick answers my question with so much gentleness packed behind his words. I can tell he's trying to show me it's okay I don't understand these things. He's not judging me for my lack of knowledge of the political machinations of men with too much power.

"Power? I don't understand."

"The United States is the most powerful nation in the world," he replies. "If you take that power and money away and you distribute it equally under the guise of 'leveling the playing field for all nations,' you weaken the strongest player but you also leave them ripe for the picking."

"What does that mean?"

"They're trying to create a one world nation," Wes adds.

"Someone else would have control over the US," Rick finishes.

"That sounds…"

"Terrifying?" Wes finishes for me. "Yeah, I agree."

"Yeah," I say. "I think I liked it better when I had no idea what was going on in the world."

"So what were you doing before the kidnappers contacted you?" Wes asks me, effectively changing the subject. Rick shoots him a look I don't quite understand, but I think they could see I was beginning to panic.

"I was styling Grace for her events this week."

"And what events were those?"

"She has a few community outreach visits and a state dinner," I answer.

"So I'm guessing Jake cut her schedule?" Wes asks.

"No, actually, we decided this afternoon that everything should go as planned, and we'll see if we can't ferret out the perpetrators," Rick says. I guess this is what they hashed out while I was sleeping the day away. I hate that I've missed so much.

"So are you guys going to pretend you're still at odds?" Wes asks, and I can't help but think it's a valid question.

"Fuck no," Rick answers, startling me and making Wes smile.

"Do you think that's wise?" I ask. I don't agree or disagree; I just want to know his reasoning. Also, the thought of forcing the hand of the people who have our only child scares the shit out of me.

"I don't care," he says, making me bristle at his callous tone. "Hear me out. They have taken enough from us. I am done pretending I don't care about you."

"Okay," I reply quietly. He says he *cares* about me. Before, Wes was sure he still loved me. I can't help but feel a flush of disappointment flow through me.

"And I want the perpetrators to show their hand. I

want them to lead me to Rachel."

"Sounds like someone's going to a State Dinner." Wes smirks, looking directly at me.

"What? No," I hurry to answer. "I dress people for the fancy dinners. I don't go to them."

"You went to the Inaugural Ball," Rick adds unhelpfully.

"And how did that end?" I snap.

"With you angry and fucking me in your hotel room." Rick laughs.

"And that's my cue to go," Wes says. "I head home in a couple of days, so let me know if you need anything."

"Don't be a stranger," Rick tells him.

"Thanks, man." Wes turns to look at me. "Oh and Cara?"

"Yeah?" I answer.

"I've changed my mind about you."

"Thanks," I say softly. "I've changed my mind about me too."

"Good," he replies before seeing himself out.

"What was that all about?" Rick asks me.

"What? Oh nothing," I answer. "Besides, you already heard it all while you were eavesdropping at the door."

"That's true," he says with a smile, making me laugh and swat his arm at the same time. "Ready for bed?"

"Yeah."

Rick takes my hand in his and leads me upstairs to the master bedroom. He draws his gun from behind his back and places it on the nightstand. He's so at ease with it that I had honestly forgotten he was carrying it until now. I watch as he strips off his jeans and T-shirt before tossing them in the hamper, and then I turn and head for the bathroom.

I start pulling open drawers until I find a spare toothbrush. I open the package and brush the pizza off my teeth. I use his man soap to wash my makeup off and use his comb to pull the snarls out of my hair.

Rick saunters into the bathroom before selecting his own toothbrush from the cup on the counter and brushing his teeth. The close quarters and intimacy of the moment coupled with Wes's revelations has me on edge, so I quickly leave the room and head back to the bedroom. I turn off the lights, pull back the light gray covers, and climb in.

I quickly roll to my side and close my eyes, pretending to be asleep when I see the bathroom light click off just before Rick emerges from the bathroom. I am the coward Wes accused me of being.

I feel the bed dip behind me, and as Rick curls his body into mine, his front presses against my back. He buries his face in my hair and stays there for a long moment. I hold my breath and wonder if he's planning to sleep in the rabbit warren that is my long, dark hair.

And then his hand skates up underneath the large T-shirt that covers my body—his T-shirt. Rick's large palm covers my breast, his calloused thumb making slow, lazy circles around the hard tip. I feel his erection grow and pulse against my backside as he continues to caress me.

Rick slides his other hand under me on the bed and then around to the front of my body. He pauses, placing an open-mouth kiss to the crook of my neck before trailing his mouth up, up, up to touch the shell of my ear with the tip of his tongue, making me gasp.

And then his hand at my side dips into the front of my borrowed sweatpants and down farther, underneath my panties. He's mere seconds away from finding out I am not asleep and that I want him with every fiber of my being. He flicks the tip of his finger back and forth against my clit. Rick growls low in the back of his throat when he feels how wet I am for him.

He tucks his face in the side of my neck, right next to my ear, as he works my clit over.

And then he lets me know I'm not fooling anyone, but I'm too far gone in my need for him to care.

"Baby," he whispers, his voice harsh against my ears with his own need for me. "I need you."

"Yes," I moan.

"I need you to let me love you," he says as he rolls me to my back. "I need you to let me into your light."

"Yes," I pant as moisture pools between my legs.

"Let me make love to you," he pleads, and I reach for him. I couldn't stop myself even if I wanted to, which I do not.

"Please, Rick," I whisper into the dark. "I need you."

And then he slides the sweatpants and my panties down my legs, leaving his thick socks on my feet. He reaches over and slides open the drawer to the nightstand, and I think he's reaching for a condom, but he doesn't. The room is dark, so I don't see what he grabbed, and I don't have time to worry about it. He shuts the drawer and rolls onto me, covering my body with his.

I feel the blunt tip of him against my center, and I tip my hips up, taking no more than the very tip of him inside me, making Rick groan.

"I need you," he whispers as he slides in deep.

"I need you too."

He was right earlier this evening when he said that life was about grabbing onto the little moments when you can. The darkness would consume us if we don't. I don't know what's going to happen tomorrow, but tonight, I have Rick, and he has me.

I wrap my arms and legs around him as he begins to really move. But it's not a rough fuck like usual; it's exactly what he asked for. Rick makes love to me, worshiping my body as he slides in and out. I gasp, the breath sawing in and out of my lungs through this push and pull between us.

I won't last long like this, but then I think, *Neither will Rick.*

He gently unwraps my arms from around his shoulders and holds each of my hands in his on either side of my head as he rocks his body into mine. And I watch the tendons in his neck ripple as I gasp, my climax rolling over me gently but completely, and he pushes in deep one last time and follows me over the edge.

Rick lets me take a decent amount of his weight, and I want it. I'll gladly take it and cherish this moment. I will love him for as long as we have, but we're in the middle of a crazy plot of outside sources, so who knows what the next day will bring. So if this is all we'll have, I'll be happy, but tonight, I decided I will always try for more.

Rick finally lets go of my hands as he sits back on his knees. And all the breath in my lungs seizes when I notice my diamond band on his pinky finger. He slides it off his finger then lifts my left hand and slides it onto mine, and for the second time tonight, he rocks me to my very soul.

"You're mine, Cara," he says quietly. "And I think tonight you finally realized you always will be. There were times I wanted to throw them in the river, but I didn't. I couldn't. These meant something to me, and in my heart, I knew they meant something to you, and you left them behind for a reason—so I kept them close to me. And every night since you came back into my life, I've hoped there would be a time I could give them back to you."

"Rick," I whisper as hot tears trail down my face.

"So here's the first one," he continues after he places a kiss to his ring back on my finger again. "You're mine, and everyone should know it. I'll give you the second one back when you're ready, when our daughter is under our roof. I'm going to give you the world. I'm going to give you both the family you should have had all along. And if we have more children, that's great, but if we don't, then that's fine with me too, because we will have Rachel. I'm going to give it all to you, if you'll let me. Will you let me, Cara?"

"Yes," I answer softly, and it's the only answer I could give him.

"Thank you."

Rick lies back down on the bed, pulling me into his arms. I rest my head on his shoulder and just let him hold me while I cry, but this time it's not heartbreaking sobs but tears of hope and joy. I finally have Rick back, and he is just as determined as I am to find our daughter. And if I just believe in him, maybe we can have it all.

He soothes me quietly for hours and then finally, when I can't cry anymore, Rick holds me tight while I drift off to sleep and dream beautiful dreams of what could be.

And in the days to come, I would find out I was wrong to hope, because hope is a bitch, and she always gets her pound of flesh.

DOES THE PRESIDENT HAVE A DIRTY LITTLE SECRET?

Rumors of Jeffries Liaison Spiral While First Lady Glows with Pregnancy

CHAPTER 19

What a bitch

Three days later…

I'm freaking the fuck out.

Tonight is the State Dinner, and to say I'm nervous is a colossal understatement. And I'm in the residence of the White House getting ready with the First Lady and the Press Secretary like a couple sixteen-year-olds getting ready for the prom. I'm not sure how this is my life. It's kind of like I woke up one day and I was in the *Twilight Zone*.

"Can you pass me that red lip gloss?" Jules asks.

"Yeah, sure," I say, picking up the square-shaped tube and passing it over.

"Really, Jules?" Grace questions her choice with a heavy amount of judgment packed behind it that only a best friend could. "Fuck-me-red for a State Dinner?"

"Too much?" she asks me.

"Uhh… probably."

"Fuck." She sighs. "I'm trying too hard."

"Anyone in particular you're trying to impress?" Grace prompts just a little too casually to actually be casual conversation.

"Fuck you, no."

This weird moment that is so natural with these two powerful women is exactly what I needed. Grace and Jules have been my friends for a while now, but this year, they brought me into the fold. I'm one of them, and it's crazy. I'm the stylist, but now, somewhere along the way, they made me family, and it is exactly what I needed. They bring me a level of balance that my life is seriously lacking. And with Rachel missing, I need them to keep me grounded while we play pretend to smoke out the bad guys.

I'm seriously living in a James Bond movie.

"How about a smoky eye with that dress instead?" I suggest, passing her a palette of golds and dark browns that will look amazing with her dark eyes and chestnut hair.

"I love that! Thank you."

"Of course." I smile at her. She's a dab hand with makeup; that's for sure. A little style direction goes a long way with these two, and they make my life so easy.

Grace does her makeup in soft browns and pinks.

She's really enjoying the innocent pregnant mother look while Jules rocks the vixen vibe. She's let her hair down in soft waves and is going to wear the emerald-green dress I found for her with some actual emerald jewelry. She's even snuck a pair of ridiculously tall heels from her old wardrobe.

"Jake is going to paddle your ass when he sees those heels." Jules laughs, and she's not wrong.

"I see nothing," I add. "I'm not a party to this, and I am not getting fired over her shoe tantrum."

"You're fine," Grace says with a delicate laugh. "I can handle him."

"Here's hoping."

"Can you do me up?" Jules asks.

"Of course." Grace helps her zip up her dress.

She's wearing a red lace dress with a mock neck, but what should be modest is... not. The entire thing is fitted through her hips and then flows to the ground. She has nude heels underneath it, and her hair twisted into elegant curls and then rolled up and pinned at the back of her neck. She looks gorgeous.

My own dress is much simpler. It has a fitted long-sleeved bodice with a neckline that just barely shows my collarbones. The back, however, dips almost to my waist. A soft organza skirt flows around my legs, making me feel like a ballerina. I twisted my long dark hair up into an intricate bun and did my makeup in dark browns and soft pinks. I love fashion and makeup, but I'm meant to be behind the scenes, not star in the show, so the more subdued style appeals to me, even though I feel like I could crap my pants or pass out at any moment. Oh, God. What if I throw up on a Japanese dignitary?

"What are you thinking about so hard over there?" Grace asks me when she notices I've gone silent.

"That I will throw up on a Japanese dignitary and humiliate myself in front of everyone ever," I admit like word vomit; they just come up and out against my own volition.

Jules laughs. "The Japanese won't even be here to-night, so you're safe."

"Thanks," I mutter.

"You'll be fine," she says as she wraps her arm around my shoulders. "We got your back. Right, fancy pants?"

"Hell yeah!" Grace laughs. "I would hug you, but my arms are no longer long enough to reach past my enormous body."

"How far along are you again?" Jules asks with a twinkle in her eye. We both agree Grace has to be the most beautiful pregnant woman alive.

"Seven hundred days." She sighs. "I think this isn't a baby and it's actually an African elephant."

"That will make the delivery entertaining," I say with a wink.

"You're both terrible." Grace laughs too. "You're both supposed to disagree with me and feel sorry for me."

"The only thing I feel sorry about is that your ass looks better than mine," Jules says.

"You say the sweetest things." Grace sighs. "All right, I'll keep you both."

Grace and Jules make me smile. It feels weird. I feel like I should never smile again. My life without Rachel in it is like a life with no sun, only eternal darkness. It feels like all the joy has been sucked out of everything. And then I feel myself smile or share a laugh with friends. And it feels both good and wrong. Like I shouldn't be allowed to have moments like this.

I know what Rick said too. And I love him, I really do. I feel like we turned a corner the other night and there will be no coming back from it. Rick and I have lived as man and wife for the last three nights, and over the last three days and nights, I've worn the ring he gave me on our wedding day. And I don't want to take it off. It's actually the only jewelry I'm wearing tonight with my beautiful gown. I don't own anything else real, and I know Rick hates the cheap costume jewelry I wore to the Inaugural Ball. And truth be told, I don't think this dress needs anything else.

But even that's not what has me freaking the fuck out.

What has me worried, what has me conjuring up all kinds of terrible scenarios in my head are the parting words that Rick gave me as we went our separate ways in the White House so I could come and dress with the girls.

As we were getting ready to say goodbye for the afternoon, Rick pulled me into his arms and kissed me stupid. When he slid back, I wore the stupidest grin on my face. And then he tucked his face in the crook of my neck for a snuggle, where he whispered in my ear words that were like a bucket of ice water being dropped on my head.

"Don't trust Black," he said.

"W-what?" I whispered.

"I don't trust him, and you shouldn't either."

"But he works for the president." Surely, we could trust the most senior military advisor to the President of the United States, right? I mean, don't they vet those people extensively?

"I didn't pick him, so I don't trust him, not with you, not with our daughter," he warned.

"I'm scared."

"Don't be," he said. "I'll be with you the whole time. Even if you can't see me, I'll have eyes on you."

"Well that's not creepy at all, ex-husband." I squeaked when he swatted me on the ass.

"Drop the ex."

"I tried. He keeps coming back."

"Not funny."

"I know." I sighed.

"Now tell me you love me," he said, pulling me

closer.

"I love you."

"Now tell me you'll be a good girl," he rumbled, his voice turning husky and sexy. I didn't say anything at all. "Cara?"

"I don't make promises I can't keep."

He rolled his eyes at me, but they still crinkled in the corners in that way I love so much. He touched his mouth to mine. It was light and firm, and he kept his eyes open to look at mine. And then it was over far too quickly.

And then I squeaked when he swatted me again and said, "Off with you."

And I haven't seen him since. Grace said he's around here somewhere smoking cigars and drinking whiskey with Jake and Ryan, but that only makes me even more nervous. I can't tell Jules and Grace what Rick said, because what if we're wrong? But then again, what if we're right and he's the bad guy? And when did my life become a spy novel? This is way too stressful.

And I thought New Jersey was bad!

I press my hand flat against my belly and take a deep breath. I need to calm my nerves, but I'm so afraid that everyone will see I'm a big fraud. That I don't belong in this life and that I'm only searching for my daughter.

"Come in," Grace says, when there's a knock at

the door.

Jake and Rick walk through the door. I notice Jules looks up like she's expecting someone, but when no one shows, she busies herself with clipping a large dangling earring through her ear.

Jake makes no effort to hide the affection he has for his wife as he wraps his arms around her and kisses her stupid.

"My lipstick," she says when he pulls back.

"Is fixable." He winks at her.

"Hey," Rick says softly, drawing my attention away from a couple who loves each other so very deeply you wouldn't know that less than a year ago he blackmailed her into being in a relationship with him. Well, Rick did most of the blackmailing. The memory makes me realize there's a lot more to this older, wiser Rick than I realized. Maybe he does carry a darkness after all.

"Hey yourself."

"You look beautiful," he says, looking at me—I mean *really* looking at me. It's like he's seen it all, the good and the bad, and he still likes what he sees under all the paint and spackle.

"Thank you."

"I brought you something," he says, looking a little nervous, and I wonder what has him so anxious and… unsteady. It's so unlike him.

"What is it?"

Rick doesn't say anything but produces a small velvet box from the inside pocket of his suit jacket. He holds out the tiny package like it's a rattlesnake about to strike, and the thought makes me smile. I gently lift it from his hands and crack open the hard shell. Nestled on a satin pillow inside are a pair of large diamond earrings with two small circles of tiny, shimmery diamonds around them.

"They're beautiful," I say. "Thank you."

"The lady in the shop called them lovers' knots, and I liked that," he says as he plucks them from their safe little slot. He gently tips my head to the side to expose my ear, and he slips the stud through before turning me to the other side.

"Why's that?" I think he's going to tell me something sweet like our hearts will always be connected or that we were always meant to be, but he does not.

"Because I like the idea of you tied up again." He smirks, making me laugh.

"You're terrible."

"I know, but I'm still yours," he says, sounding more than a little unrepentant but still in a way that is romantic in his own way.

"It's time, Mr. President," Gus says from the doorway. He must have knocked when I wasn't paying attention.

"Ready?"

"I'm as ready as I'll ever be." I sigh.

"Don't look so down." Rick winks at me, showing me a hint of the happy-go-lucky guy I married almost a decade ago. "You have the best-looking date in the room.

"You're supposed to say I'm the best-looking date, silly!"

"Oh," he says, faking an affronted look. "My apologies."

"Goober," I reply, rolling my eyes. "I guess we need to go."

But when we turn to leave the room, I notice everyone is watching us, and they all have differing silly expressions on their faces.

"What?" I whisper-snap to Grace, but she just shakes her head very subtly before taking Jake's arm and walking from the room.

AS IT TURNS OUT, official State Dinners are funny things.

Because of Rick's status as Chief of Staff, we were afforded pretty fancy seating at a table with a party of the foreign dignitaries' entourages. My only saving grace was that Jules is apparently of the same caliber as Rick in the grand scheme of political hierarchy, so she was at our table and seated directly next to me. I'm sure Grace had a lot to do with that table assignment, and I'm sorry Jules got stuck at the table babysitting me. Not that she made me feel that way at all.

The downside of that is that Captain Black is also apparently of this political echelon and seated several seats over from Jules. His nearness keeps me on edge, and Rick drops his hand to the top of my thigh underneath the table to distract me. He is so in tune with me, and I with him. And I swear I can feel his fingertip at the edge of my panties even through the million layers of my skirt. The distraction helps ease my mind.

I'm actually surprised that all the people closest to the president are seated at a different table. Although there are a lot of people here tonight. More people than I ever thought imaginable, and I was at the Inaugural Ball.

I quietly pick through course after course of dinner. Jules talks to me some, but her job is to entertain the rest of our table, as is Rick's and Captain Black's. I answer when I'm asked a question and smile when I need to, but I'm really unnecessary at this event, which is great, because on the inside I'm dying slowly.

I'm just the date of the Chief of Staff. Actually, I'm not even sure what I am to him. I know that I'm his ex-wife and the mother of his daughter. I know that I'm currently his lover and wearing his ring, but what that means, I have no idea.

After dinner, we're free to move about the cabin.

Grace and Jake open up the dance floor, which I have learned is actually part of her official duties. The whole thing is wild. I stand dutifully beside Rick as he works the room. Every so often, he reaches for my hand or the small of my back, nothing too forward or inappropriate for the room, but it's a grounding touch, like he needs to know I'm still there.

"Mind if I steal your girl for a minute?" Jules asks Rick after a while. I can see he wants to say no, that I need to be beside him where he can get to me if I need him. It's not a controlling thing, and I know that if our daughter wasn't missing right now, I would be free to do whatever I wanted. Hell, I probably wouldn't even be here right now; I'd be home with Rachel. It's another little tell of Rick's that he's feeling out of control and doesn't like it. I don't think anyone else spots it, but Jules is very perceptive. So I shouldn't be surprised when she lowers her voice and whispers for his ears only, "She'll be safe. I promise. And Ryan is close."

His dark eyes flare, and then he surprises me when he answers, "Sure. Don't be gone too long." And then he places a hard and fast kiss to my lips before letting me go and turning away.

Jules wraps my arm around hers and leads me to a darker corner of the room where people don't seem to be hanging around, grabbing each of us a glass of champagne from a passing waiter on the way by. She's like a dancer the way she moves with so much grace and class. I can almost see her as a girl Rachel's age, walking around the house with an encyclopedia on her head.

"How are you holding up?" she asks me as she hands me a glass of champagne.

"I think I'm doing all right," I answer before taking a sip of my drink.

"I know you're nervous, but you're doing marvelous," she assures.

"Really?" I ask incredulously. "Because it feels like I've said three words the whole night and only spoke when asked something."

"Yes! That's exactly what the group wants," she says, rolling her eyes. "Women aren't supposed to speak."

"Then why are you?" I sip more of my champagne. I'm fascinated by this side of Jules. I've always seen her as a dear friend of Grace's. She's kind and witty, and Lord knows she's gorgeous, but right now, she's in her element, and it's awesome to see her come alive like this.

"Because it irritates them." She winks.

"No, you do not." I gasp.

"Oh, I totally do. Everyone knows it too." She sips her champagne as well.

"And they just let you get away with it?" I ask. God bless Julia Fairchild for being the kind of woman who will seek out a new friend in need in a ridiculously fancy State Dinner, when she is probably needed elsewhere, to make said new friend laugh and relax, even if it's just for a little bit. I like her. I'm keeping her.

"Mostly." She shrugs until something across the room catches her eye, making her scowl. I look over my shoulder to where she's looking and see Captain Black looking absolutely frustrated and more than a little murderous. I'm not going to lie; his expression has me shrinking back just a bit. "Well, except for Ryan. He doesn't seem to approve of me very much."

"I'm sorry," I whisper.

Jules just shrugs it off. "Don't be. I'm not."

"I like you, Julia Fairchild," I tell her, making her laugh again. "I'm keeping you."

"Oh good," she says with a broad smile. "Because I've already decided to keep you too."

"Fantastic news."

"Oh dear, Grace is sending up a Romeo," she says, looking away from Captain Black but still across the room.

"She's sending up a what?" I ask, looking to where she seems to be focused.

"See how she's sliding the pendant on her necklace back and forth while glancing over here every so often?" she asks me.

"Yes, I do," I answer. "What is she doing? She looks a little ridiculous."

"She does, doesn't she?" Jules replies. "She's sending up a Romeo. It's an old sorority secret. When you need an out, you slide your necklace like that, and a sister or two will come rescue you. Simple as that. So, you see, it's our duty to go find out what our dear First Lady needs."

"Seeing as how she's very pregnant and dancing a bit, I'm guessing it's the powder room," I suggest.

"It looks like you would be correct."

"We should probably hurry."

"Hello!" Jules says brightly, interrupting whatever the man she was speaking to was saying. "Will you excuse us for a moment? I need to steal the First Lady for some important business."

She doesn't give the man a chance to reply; she just steers Grace away and through the door and down the hall. It's actually one of the more impressive maneuvers I've seen her execute in the entire time I've known her.

We bypass a ladies' room and travel farther down the hall. Grace's main agent follows us at a discreet distance. We take a turn down another hallway and find a more private restroom. A quick look shows it's empty.

"Thank God," Grace exclaims rather dramatically, although I remember what it was like to have a baby sitting on your bladder like that, so I get it. "Jake's giant baby is Irish folk dancing on my now very teeny tiny bladder. I thought I was going to die."

"Well, we're all glad you didn't," Jules says.

I smirk at her in the gold-framed mirror. It takes

a brave woman to throw shit at the First Lady of the United States. Granted, they've been friends since they were freshman in college, so they've probably seen each other through a world of shit. The thought makes my heart pang. While they had each other, I had no one. But now I have them. Thank God for that.

Grace comes out of the stall and washes her hands. As she's reapplying her lipstick, two women walk in the restroom, laughing and clearly enjoying themselves.

"Did you see the way Jake was looking at you?" the blonde asks. "He clearly can't wait to get his hands on you, and who could blame him? His wife is the size of a barn."

"And I can't wait for him to get his hands on me." The redhead laughs. "He's so good with his hands."

They come around the corner and see us standing there. I barely keep from rolling my eyes. Actually, I don't think I was very successful at it, because the redhead narrows her beady little eyes at me. This was a mean-girl ambush if ever I saw one, and I should know; I have an eight-year-old daughter, and even she's a better orchestrator than these idiots.

"Oh!" The redhead gasps in mock horror. "You weren't supposed to hear that."

"You don't say," Grace drawls.

"I never wanted you to find out about us this way," she carries on, and it's the most ridiculous show of theatrics I have ever seen.

"Sure, sure," Grace says.

"It's just that you know Jake and I have known each other for so long, and our families go way back. One thing just kind of led to another," she says. "You know how it is."

I kind of wonder if Grace is going to rip her hair out for insinuating that Jake is having an affair with this piece of trash. Hell, I kind of want to rip her hair out, but I'm a guest of an important person at the White House, so that's probably frowned upon. I'm just about to open my mouth to suggest we find somewhere else to go, when Jules laughs. She doesn't just laugh; she snickers that little laugh of someone clearly trying to hold it in and then inch by inch, giggle by giggle, she's bent over in full-blown belly laughs.

"I don't see what's so funny," the redhead snaps.

"You are," Jules says, wiping a tear from her eye. "Like anyone would believe that load of horse shit that just spewed from your mouth. Everyone can see Jake is madly in love with his wife. You're just mad it's not you after the military campaign you waged last year for his ring. Right, Cara?"

"Right," I laugh awkwardly, but I think I cover it well in the name of the sisterhood and all that. "Jake is full gone for Grace. Anyone can see that. The thought of him cheating is laughable at best. Good one."

"I wouldn't be so quick to laugh if I were you," she says, turning on me. "Amy was talking to Rick earlier, and he was very interested. If you know what I mean."

"Oh, I do, and I'm not worried." I am. It's a lie. I wonder all the time what he's doing with me. Especially after all I have put him through. But when I think about his never taking another woman to his bed, I know that maybe we have a chance, if everything works out like it's supposed to. Besides, this chick is just a bitch. What do I care what she thinks? I have enough of my own garbage going around in my head.

"We should probably get going, ladies," Grace says to Jules and me. "Nice seeing you again, Ashley."

"Don't think you'll keep him!" she whisper-hisses as we leave. "He will come back to me. He always comes back to me." And then the door closes, cutting off her venomous tirade.

"Wow," I whisper. "What a bitch."

We wind our way back through the crowd, and Jake steals Grace away, their duty for the evening done. Jules and I say goodnight, and then Rick materializes beside me. The way he moves so quietly always surprises me.

"Ready to go?" he asks me.

"I thought you'd never ask," I reply, making Jules laugh.

"Be good, kids," she says, kissing me on the cheek, and then she too is gone.

Rick leads me out to the town car that is waiting to take us home. He loads me up inside and takes me back to his house. I don't even think about going to my own empty home. There's nothing there for me without Rick and Rachel. He's somehow cemented my life and his together in just a few days.

He thanks the driver and leads me into the house. My feet are killing me, and I can't wait to take my shoes off. It's a shame to drop three-thousand-dollar shoes by the door, but I literally can't go another step with them on my feet tonight.

Rick takes my hand in his and leads me up the stairs to his bedroom. Gently, tenderly, we undress each other, carefully folding our fancy clothes in neat piles or draping them over the bench at the foot of the bed.

And only when we both stand before each other with ourselves completely laid bare does he lead me to the bed, where he makes love to me in a way that he never has before, with a passion so wild and a love that is felt soul-deep.

And when we both find completion held tight in each other's arms, Rick tucks the covers around us, and I fall asleep safely in his arms, never knowing it would probably be the last time, because he had a plan in place to change the game and smoke out the kidnappers, and for that lack of knowledge, I was going to die.

POTUS AND FLOTUS SPEND PEACEFUL SUNDAY WITH POWERFUL FRIENDS

CHAPTER 20

Everything changed

ere's the thing about last days. Unless you're on death row, you never know yours is coming.

Otherwise, you would have had pancakes instead of oatmeal for breakfast or maybe even ice cream. You would make love one more time, maybe with the windows open in the early morning so that you can smell the coming rain.

Maybe you say goodbye to family and friends and tell them how much they mean to you. Or you go out and spend a boatload of money that you didn't have—or maybe you did.

Or you would dance in the rain.

There are so many things I could have done differently, but in the end, I wouldn't have changed a thing.

This morning, Rick woke me with his hand moving between my thighs. By the time my eyes opened and I knew what was happening, I was wet and needy, my climax rapidly barreling down on me, and there was no stopping it.

"Rick, please," I begged. "I need you."

And then he positioned his cock at my entrance and drove deep inside me.

Lately, Rick had been gentle and tender with me, always loving, but the way he fucked me this morning spoke volumes of the way everything has changed. Something was riding him hard, and he expended the energy that had woken him early this morning by joining our bodies with a fierce desperation.

Other than my initial plea for him, no words were spoken between us, but then again, I guess there didn't need to be. With every plunge into my waiting body, Rick showed me how much he needed me. He told me without words how important I am to him. And in kind, I showed him the same with the way I clung to him, how my hips rose up to meet his with a wildness we both felt, that he was it for me. There would never be anyone for me like Rick.

My climax didn't wash over me gently but seemed to detonate every molecule of my being. My entire world was spinning out of control and my tether to the here and now was where Rick's body was joined with my own.

I felt him swell inside me before he planted himself

deep and let out a rough groan while he found his own bliss within me.

He dropped his forehead down to mine and closed his eyes. This was it. This was right. I never should have denied Rick. I should have trusted him then and now. We were always meant to be together. We're like the earth and the moon, always circling each other, never able to escape the pull of the other. He is my partner, my lover, my everything, and I will never not trust him again.

"I love you," he said, his voice thick with unspoken emotion and gruff-sounding.

"I love you," I whispered back.

He pulled me tighter into his arms before releasing me. I missed him immediately as he pulled out and got up and headed for the shower. I should've known that something was amiss. Instead, I lazed in bed while he showered. I trusted him to tell me when things changed.

What I didn't know was that I while was welcoming him home with my body, my heart, my very soul, Rick was saying goodbye with his.

WHERE IS WHITE HOUSE CHIEF OF STAFF'S DAUGHTER?

CHAPTER 21

A lie

I feel restless.

The house is full of people. I thought Rick and I would spend the day together, talking about what needed to be done. I wanted to tell him my thoughts in private about reaching out to the kidnapper again. Maybe I could talk to them, find out something, anything, but once again, he had other plans he didn't share with me.

It's hard to trust someone who doesn't offer you the tools to do so. I'm struggling to rationalize the man who demands I give him my complete blind faith in his ability to save our daughter. He wants me to trust him to get the job done, but at the same time, he gives me nothing in return.

This morning, I jumped in the shower after he walked out with a towel slung low around his narrow hips. I thought we would talk today and be honest with each other, but I was wrong.

While I was in the shower, Rick was busy making phone calls and putting his own plans in place. And when I came downstairs in leggings and a T-shirt, the house was full of people.

"We brought takeout," Captain Black says as he and Jules walk in the front door. The house is already filled with Jake and Grace, Joe and Gus, and Wes. I've clearly missed a lot while my head was in the clouds.

"And coffee," she adds. "Lots and lots of coffee."

"What's all this?" I ask, and Grace cringes.

I can tell by the look on her face that she knew this was coming last night and kept the truth from me. All it takes is one look around the room to realize they all knew, and no one said a goddamned thing. My face heats with embarrassment. I always knew I didn't belong in this tight-knit crowd. This group of wealthy, powerful people, and me, the girl who grew up poor in foster care, the one puzzle piece that never quite fit.

The hot tears from this unbearable realization sting the backs of my eyes. They all see it. I never hid a damn thing from them while I was playing pretend. Pretending I didn't love Rick. Pretending I could have it all. I've spent the last few days living in his house and forgetting that in the end I wouldn't have a goddamned thing.

I rub the back of my hand against my temple where a pulse is begging to throb.

"Can I get you a cup of coffee, honey?" Jules asks gently.

"No," I answer just a little too sharply to be believable as anything I tried to pass off, and we all know it, so I give them the partial truth. "I have a headache. I think I had just a little too much champagne last night."

"Okay, but—" she starts, and I can't let her finish. I'll lose it. I'll lose my tight hold on the control I have on my emotions. I can't cry in front of these people who aren't bad people; they're just not my people, and they never were. It's not their fault they've had each other for a lifetime, and I've had no one. I have to let them go without making them feel guilty for it.

"I'm just going to lie down," I say quickly. "Let me know if you need me."

I turn and look at Rick, my words holding more meaning for him. He stands the farthest away from where I am, casually leaning against the counter. He watches me. Rick watches every damn move I make. He watches me struggle to breathe, to get out of the room fast enough.

And he doesn't say one word to stop me.

I take three steps casually, and then as soon as I'm out of their sight, I scurry up the stairs like a little rat. I hate it. I hate this is me, but *it is me*. This is what I do; I run.

I make it into the master bedroom, and I quickly lock the door behind me. I couldn't bear it if someone saw me so pathetically broken and alone. I need to emerge from this with at least some tiny shreds of my dignity and pride left so I can find my daughter and leave. Maybe we'll settle in New Mexico this time. Or even Sedona. I hear the desert is beautiful in winter.

But is it fair to take Rachel from her father? Again. It's not, and in my head, I know that. My broken heart has absolutely nothing to do with his ability as a dad.

I look around and see Rick's domain. The dark furniture and gray bedding. The lack of bright color and decoration. There's a handful of my stuff around the room, but that's it. My lotion on the bedside table with my cell phone plugged into the charger. My bright floral-print robe is draped over the chair in the corner, and the earrings he gave me sit in a little floral ceramic dish on the dresser.

Seeing them reminds me of all he said and did to show me that we were an us.

And it was all a lie.

My hands shake as I raise them up in front of me. My breath is thready as it saws in and out of my chest, and the tear I held back in the kitchen spills and rolls down my cheek. Another follows quickly on its heels.

And then with my thumb and index finger, I slide the gold and diamond band off my forever finger. It was never meant to wear any adornment there. I'm not meant to belong to anyone or have anyone belong to me.

I drop it in the bowl with the beautiful earrings and all the promises they held and let the rest of my heart shatter.

I look over my shoulder to the bed that this morning felt like it held so much love and promises between two people who were devoted to each other. Now, it feels like it was just another stack of lies and unkept promises.

I look back to the door. It stands there like a heavy symbol of the wall between the two camps, the dichotomy between everyone and me. I could straighten myself out and go back out there. I could continue to pretend they aren't all lying to me. That they care about me and my daughter, when their loyalties lie with Rick and Rick alone.

Even the idea of going back out there makes my stomach turn. I can't handle it. I know I can't. I can't go back there and watch them all watching me, so I turn back to the bed and climb in. The pillows smell like Rick's aftershave, and I pull one into my chest and hold it tight, because in my heart of hearts, I know holding him again isn't an option. We can't keep lying to each other the way we were. It hurts too much. We're going to have to figure out the co-parenting thing when we get Rachel back, but after that, no.

Was Captain Black ever a bad guy, or was it just another opportunity to keep an eye on me?

I pull the covers over my head just in time for the first sob to bubble up to the surface. It hurts so much. Loving someone shouldn't hurt.

I hold my breath when I hear footsteps on the stairs.

I don't want anyone to bother me. I can't bear to face them right now. Maybe not ever.

The doorknob rattles.

"It's locked," I hear Grace whisper followed by a light knock on the door.

"Honey, are you all right?" Rick asks softly. His tone makes me feel like he cares, but in my head and in my heart, I know it's a lie. I don't need Maury Povich to open the results to know he's full of shit.

I don't answer them.

"Do you think she's all right?" Grace asks him.

"She'll be fine," he answers tersely. "She's probably just sleeping. It was a late night last night."

"But don't you think we should have told her…" Grace's voice trails off.

"Absolutely not," Rick says. "She has enough on her mind."

Oh, I have plenty on my mind. I want to throw open the door and tell them both what a bag of dicks they all are for keeping shit from me. Making me trust them when they never trusted me. But I don't.

"But Rick—"

"Just leave it alone," he snaps.

A short while later, I hear their footsteps retreat down the stairs where I'm left with my thoughts. I wonder if I got Grace alone if she'd admit to me what's really going on. Or has she been suitably warded from doing so by Rick and his merry band of asshole buddies. It sucks when the man who wants to keep you in the dark is the same one who is friends with some of the most powerful people in the world.

I wipe my eyes with the back of my hand. I wonder if I could sneak down the stairs and get her attention before everyone else noticed me. Could I separate her from the group and get some much-needed information out of her?

But I don't get to put my plan into motion, because my phone rings.

And when I answer it, everything changes.

NEW FROM THE HILL: CONTROVERSIAL BILL WILL BE REINTRODUCED MONDAY

CHAPTER 22

Backfire

"Hello?" I whisper into my phone.

When it rang, I snatched it up off the nightstand and slid my finger over the glass to unlock it as fast as I could. Everyone I know is here in this house, so the only person who would be calling me is the kidnapper. And I need to talk to them. I'll do whatever it takes to get Rachel back, even if it's to a life that no longer has me in it.

"I thought you would have learned your lesson by now," the robotic voice says.

"I did," I whisper furiously. "I did. I'll do whatever you say."

"Then why are you living with Mr. Donovan?" the voice asks.

"He won't let me go," I admit and decide that sticking as close to the truth as possible can't hurt. "He's angry with me for keeping his daughter from him, and now he won't let me go home."

"An interesting predicament for sure," he says, and then I hear two loud booms in the distance. "I guess you should figure something out."

"Take me," I say before I can think it through. "Take me instead. But let my daughter go."

"I'll think about it," the voice lies to me, and we both know it. They have no intention of letting her go. I can only hope she hasn't been harmed yet while I was playing Rick's deadly games. "I guess you'll have to find us first." And then he hangs up.

"No!" I shout but then look around. I can't afford to have anyone hear me and stop me from going and getting my daughter.

I know where she is.

The realization hits me like a ton of bricks, making me gasp. She's been close the whole time. The whole fucking time my daughter has been no more than three blocks away. I know, because the two loud booms are very familiar. They are the same noise as the double backfire of Amber's old minivan whenever she parks. In fact, I'm willing to bet it's the exact same sound, because the kidnappers are keeping Rachel somewhere close to Amber's house.

She had mentioned before when I felt like I couldn't live right next door to Rick that her neighbors had moved out and were looking for tenants, but when

I finally asked about it in a moment of weakness, she said it was already taken. I don't want to call her and put her in danger. That's not fair to Amber, her daughter Becky, or her husband Aaron. I would never do that to her or to anyone.

I can't tell the group where I'm going. I don't trust them—not anymore. But I feel like I have to leave some kind of clue as to where I'm going. A note? Maybe. I don't know. I don't like not being able to talk to them. I used to be just fine on my own, and damn Rick for making me trust him. He made me fall back in love with him... if I ever even stopped loving him in the first place.

This is so stupid.

I look around the room. He literally keeps nothing in here. There's nothing but an industrial-sized box of condoms in the nightstand drawer along with some power cables. There's nothing I could use to leave a note in the bathroom either. Where is a pen and a pad of paper when you need one? Doesn't everybody have like seven hundred free notepads from realtors? I swear in my house I have them coming out of my ears!

That's it! My house! I need to get to my house, and I can leave a note and grab my keys and drive to Amber and Aaron's neighborhood.

I toss back the covers and climb out of bed. This morning, I threw on leggings with a floral print all over them and a black V-neck T-shirt over a pink tank top. I like the comfy layered look. It hides my love handles. So now, I just need a pair of sneakers and a jacket.

I slide my feet into a pair of Converse and grab my denim jacket.

Now, to escape next door.

Quietly, I turn the lock on the door and slowly twist the knob. I hold my breath, terrified to make a noise and be found. I tiptoe down the stairs. I pause at the bottom of the stairs just before they open up into the kitchen. I wait and listen. And then I peek my head around the corner. The room is empty.

I scurry into the kitchen and hear voices coming from the living room at the front of the house.

I have to move quickly.

"We should have heard from them by now," Rick says, and I can hear the frustration in his voice.

"We will," Captain Black says. "You have to let the plan work."

They have a plan. That's just fucking great. It would have been nice if they told me about the plan, since it involved me and my daughter. I don't stay to find out what they're talking about. I walk straight to the kitchen door that leads out into the side yard where the trashcans are stored. Rick's house is a mirror image of my own, so I know I can walk around to my garage from there.

The deadbolt sounds like a gunshot in my ears when I flip the lock open, and I freeze, hoping no one heard anything. I open the door and step out, shutting it quietly behind me, breathing a sigh of relief. I've made it this far, so there's no going back now.

I skirt my overhead garage door down to the far side where there is a digital keypad to open the door with a code. Thank God Rick insisted on digital locks being installed all over both houses so that we would be safe.

Spoiler alert: we weren't safe anyway, but I will be able to get my car and leave. And that's exactly what I do.

Once the overhead door is high enough I can get underneath it, I do and head straight for the door into my house. I race to the kitchen and grab a notepad from a realtor named Remy, and I pen a quick note to Rick.

Rick,

I know where Rachel is. She's being kept in a house over by Amber's house. They called me, and I heard her car in the background. I think I can get them to exchange her for me. I knew you would try to stop me, so I didn't tell you, but if something happens, I need you to make sure our daughter is safe. Give her a beautiful life.

—Cara

I leave the note stuck to the pad of paper and the pen with it on the kitchen counter of the island. I can only hope Rick will see it. Rachel knows where

Becky's house is. If I can get her out, I'll send her to Amber and have her call Rick.

And then I realize I left my phone upstairs, on the bedside table in Rick's master bedroom. I close my eyes as my frustration with myself mounts higher and higher. How could I have been so careless? I can't risk going back, so I'm going to have to leave without it and hope for the best.

I grab my keys off the hook by the door to the garage and head out. I beep the locks and climb in as fast as I can. I buckle my seat belt and look over my shoulder like I'm some kind of bank robber on the run. It takes me three tries to get the key in the ignition, because my hands are shaking so badly, but as soon as I do, I turn the key.

I back out of my driveway and head out to get my kid back. I can't believe I finally got the break I needed so badly. Here's hoping I can find her and get her out.

The drive to Amber and Aaron's neighborhood is a short one; it's really only a few blocks away. I park a few houses down on a side street and try to catch my breath.

Am I making a huge mistake?

I should have told Rick the minute I got off the phone with the kidnapper and realized I knew where she was being held. I should have trusted him, and I didn't. But then again, he didn't trust me either.

Regret burns in my belly, and I'm just about to turn the car back on and drive back to Rick's. I need to confess everything I did wrong. I can only hope Rick forgives me.

But you know what they say about hope? You can shit in one hand and hope in the other and see which fills up faster. That old saying rings through my head as there is a knock on my window. I roll it down to Amber's smiling face.

"Hey, girl," she says. "What are you doing here?"

I don't know how to answer here. I don't feel like I can say the truth. But at the same time, I might need her help. Still, I feel out the situation and do what comes naturally to me. I lie.

"I just needed to go for a drive and get some fresh air."

"Why don't you come in for a cup of coffee?" she suggests, and I know I need to get rid of her. I need to find Rachel and get her out of here.

"Oh no, thank you," I say with a smile. "I'm heading out now."

"I'm afraid I can't let you do that," she says.

And that's when she lifts her hand.

A hand that's holding a small gun, which is aimed at me.

"I think I'll take that cup of coffee after all," I say, my eyes on the gun.

"That's what I thought you'd say."

She pulls open the door to my car, and I unbuckle my seatbelt and step out of the car. I walk side by side with Amber, her gun digging into the side of my ribs.

"Why, Amber?" I ask. "I thought we were friends."

"We are," she says, and I can hear her voice waiver. This is not of her doing. "She's said she'd kill Aaron if I didn't help her."

"I'm so sorry this happened to you, Amber," I tell her with all the feeling I can put into it. Her family would be safe if she'd never met me.

"I'm so sorry this happened to you too, Cara."

"I know, honey."

"Now get into the house."

The door swings shut behind us, and Ashley Jeffries steps around the corner with another gun pointed at me.

"Surprise, bitch." She laughs just before clubbing me over the head, and as the pain blossoms out from the back of my skull, everything goes black.

NEW BROMANCE BLOSSOMS: PRESIDENT'S AIDE-DE-CAMP HANGS OUT OFF DUTY WITH POTUS AND CHIEF OF STAFF

CHAPTER 23

She's gone.

Rick

"Did you hear that?" Ryan asks, and I'm still not sure I can trust him, even though Jake says he's as solid as a brick. I didn't vet him, so I don't know.

"Hear what?" I look toward him, and he's looking toward the kitchen. He appears to be relaxed; maybe his interest is a little piqued.

"It sounded like the door opened," he says, reaching for his gun that's tucked into the back of his jeans. To anyone looking in from the outside, we're just a bunch of friends gathered to watch some ball game and eat junk food, but even though we're laughing and casually dressed, we're ready—and armed. "I'm just going to go check that out."

"Sure," I say before picking up my soda can and taking a sip.

I hate the pretense. All of this bullshit bugs me, but I know it's necessary. I just wish I could have read Cara in. I know she's up there right now, crying in my bed, the bed I made love to her in last night and this morning, and she's thinking I don't give a fuck about her. But that couldn't be further from the truth. Last night, Jake and I laid the groundwork to smoke out the perpetrators by placing a big fat target on my back.

I would do anything to make sure Cara and Rachel are safe and that they stay that way, even if it costs me my own life. So I came back home and made love to my wife one more time, knowing that today may be my last, but afterward, even if everything went to shit, she'd have our baby in her arms again.

Fuck, what I wouldn't give to get to watch my baby grow in her belly. I can only hope that everything goes to plan and, by the end of the day, we'll have our girl back and can finally get on with our lives. But you know what they say about hope.

"Hey, Rick?" Black calls out from the back of the house, and the way he says my name has the hairs standing on the back of my neck.

"Yeah?" I stay in my chair in case anyone is watching. But inside, I'm dying to prowl my house. Something is wrong with my stronghold, the place I've built to protect my family. The next words he speaks sends ice shooting through my veins.

"The side door is unlocked."

I don't say anything. I just get up from my chair and take the stairs two at a time. I know something is wrong before I ever get to the end of the hallway, because I can see that the bedroom door, which was previously shut and locked when I tried to get to Cara, is now standing ajar.

I push it open and see the bed is unmade. Cara laid down like I suspected. Did she cry over me and the way I treated her this afternoon? I scan the room and see that her engagement band is in the colorful bowl she put all of her jewelry. I know she was wearing it this morning when I woke her with my hand on her pussy, and I know she was wearing it when she walked downstairs to the see kitchen full of people this afternoon, because I always look for it. Now, it sits in the mills with the earrings I had given her just last night. I joked about the earring in front of our friends, but I could tell she knew the real meaning went deeper. And now she's left them all behind. She's left me behind.

Maybe she's in the bathroom or in the closet. I move through the master suite to look, but even before I open doors, I know she's not here. I call down the stairs the words I never wanted to say, ones I said nine years ago when I was deployed and she left me over the phone.

"She's gone!"

I don't hear a verbal reply, but I do hear a variety of footsteps pound up the stairs and fill the door of my bedroom. I don't want to look at them and admit I fucked up and it could cost me my family.

"What was that?" Jake says as Wes and Ryan prowl the room, no doubt looking for something.

"She's gone."

I don't know what to do. I drop down to sit on the edge of the bed and hold my head in my hands. I'm always sure of myself during a mission, but right now, I'm struggling. I fucked up. I demanded Cara's trust and gave her none of my own in return. I was just trying to protect her, and now it may be too late.

"What do I do now?"

"We find her," Wes says.

"She's gone, man. She left me."

"Did you let me take that shit when Grace walked out?" Jake growls.

"No."

"So are we going to take this lying down?" he asks.

"No," I say. "But how do we find her? I don't even know where to start."

"I think I do," Ryan says from the far side of the bed. He's holding up her phone in his hand. "They called her about twenty minutes ago."

"Fuck," I bite out.

"That's a twenty-minute lead," Wes states. "That's not too bad."

"And Black said he heard something in the kitchen," Jake reminds me. "And the side door was open."

"Where does the kitchen side door lead to?" Black asks.

I stand up. He's right. I have to follow her trail. Everyone follows me downstairs and into the kitchen. We go through the side door and out to where my trashcans are stored, but I have a feeling....

I turn the corner, and lo and behold, her garage door is open. I walk through the garage, not bothering to see if anyone is following me. Cara's car is gone. She would have had to go inside to grab her keys. I made sure those were not included in her belongings when I moved her into my house with me. I didn't want her to be able to run until I convinced her we were real.

I take a chance and walk into her house and look around. It looks like she didn't make it very far into the house. The living room and stairs still look as if they've been untouched since the last time I was here.

"Hey, Rick?" Jake calls out.

"What's that?"

"You might wanna come have a look at this," he says, and I follow his voice into the kitchen where sitting on the counter is a freebie notepad. It drives me crazy that Cara keeps all those shoved in a drawer. But this one is different. On the pad, in her messy handwriting, is a note telling me what she should have said to my face.

"Fuck, fuck!" I bite out and run my hands through my hair. It's a sign of my agitation that I've never been able to get rid of.

She knows where Rachel is, and she went to get her on her own. I know where the house is. I've dropped Rachel off at Becky's enough times, and now I have to go get my girls and hope to God I'm not fucking late.

I race back through the house and into my own to grab the keys to my SUV. I check the magazine in my gun and re-holster it behind my back.

What I don't do is notice Ryan Black's absence from the group. I would regret that later.

I exit through the door to the garage at the back of the house, much the same way Cara escaped her house, and I head down the road. Rachel's friend Becky and her family don't live too far from where Cara and I do. It's ten minutes at best. I only hope it's not too late.

When I drive down a side street, I notice Cara's vehicle. It's a piece of shit sedan, and when this is all over, I'll buy her the car she deserves. I'll take care of her and Rachel for the rest of my life, and I won't take no for an answer. *Just don't let me be too late.*

I don't even bother to hide I'm here. I walk right up the front porch and knock on the door. No one answers, and I knock again.

I hear a scream from somewhere in the back of the house, maybe a basement that's not sealed inside, and I kick the door in. I pull my gun from the back of my jeans and hold it loose at my side while I make my way through the house.

I think I've found where the scream came from. There's a door that sits ajar at the back just like my bedroom door had. I raise my gun and take off at a run, and then I hear a sickening crack that can only mean one thing.

SECOND CHANCE
ROMANCE: CHIEF
OF STAFF AND EX
ARE OFF THE
MARKET

CHAPTER 24

Just run

Cara

Thirty minutes earlier…

"Mommy! Mommy, you have to wake up."

I hear Rachel cry as she shakes me, and I force my eyes open. My head is pounding, and I feel like I'm going to throw up. Thank God I haven't eaten anything today or I'm sure I would've. But even though I feel absolutely terrible, I realize my daughter is here.

"Rachel!" I cry as I push myself to sit up. I've finally found her, and nothing could stop me from pulling her into my arms.

"Mommy, I was so scared!" she cries. "They said you wouldn't come, but you did."

"I did, my sunshine girl," I say softly as I brush her hair away from her face. "I told you I would always find you no matter how long it took me. I would never stop looking for you."

And that's true. Even when Rick and I were pretending like everything was fine, we were still looking for her. She was never forgotten. I look around the room where my daughter has been held for the better part of a week, and I want to scream. There's nothing terrible about the room. It's plain with a small window. There's an old daybed against the far wall and a small metal card table and chairs where she's clearly been getting her meals and coloring. There's a door that leads to a bathroom off to the right. But that's not what has me so upset.

She was so close, and I had no idea! It breaks my mothering heart to think she was so close, and I didn't know. I carried her in my body. I should have felt something!

I help Rachel stand up, and then I push to stand. The room swims before me. Ashley didn't pull any punches when she clobbered me on the head. I honestly thought she was just another spoiled socialite from the Upper East Side. I had no idea she had a homicidal streak in her. And I honestly can't see how she was behind the plot to take down the president. She's just not that smart.

I try the doorknob and it's locked. Shit! I have to get Rachel out of here. The window on the far wall is up way too high and is too narrow for me to push her out of. Not to mention, she'd get hurt falling from a window this high. We're going to have to wait for someone to come in here and open the door. Best-case scenario, I can distract them so my baby can get away.

I always knew I would trade myself for her. But actually knowing it's going to happen is terrifying. I'm not afraid to die, because I would happily trade my life for hers over and over again. I'm afraid to say goodbye to my daughter.

Now I have to explain to her what I need her to do. That I need her to run to Amber's house. I know she wouldn't have done this if she weren't afraid. But now I need her to help get my baby to safety. Rick will protect her from there and hopefully give her a beautiful life. They both deserve it.

"Come here, Rachel," I say softly. I crouch down in front of her so she can see my face. It's something I've always done when I want her to know I'm serious.

"What is it, Mom?" Her big hazel eyes, so much like her daddy's, look at me wide and scared.

"I need you to listen to me. We're in a pretty tough spot right now, but we've made it out of tough spots before, right?"

"Right," she answers me like I know all the secrets of the world and I'll never let her down. But I'm about to let her down now; she just doesn't know it yet. But I'm not walking out of this room with her. This is where my story ends.

"I'm going to get you out of here," I tell her. "But I

need you to be very brave for me."

"I know." She smiles at me.

"When I tell you to run, you run and don't look back." I weight my words so that she knows how serious they are. "Promise me, Rachel."

"I promise, Mommy."

"Don't look back," I tell her.

God, please just let her run. Don't let her hear or see anything. I need her out of this house of horrors before I die.

"I won't," she says quietly.

"It's going to be okay," I tell her.

Please, God, just let her be okay.

"Okay." She nods her little head. Her dark brown curls are a rat's nest. I hope Rick has the presence of mind to deal with combing this mess out, because she would not look good bald. This just goes to show that the things that run through your mind at the end are actually ridiculous.

"Daddy will find you."

"But what about you?" she asks me the one thing I was hoping she wouldn't ask, even though it needs to be said.

Don't cry, don't cry, don't cry...

Tears burn the back of my throat. "Don't worry about me," I say, forcing a smile I don't feel to my face. "I'll find you when it's all over."

"Mom...." God, sometimes, I hate how smart she is. Even though she's only eight, I know she can tell I'm lying. She just doesn't know about what, and I'd like to keep it that way. My sweet girl will learn soon enough.

"Just remember to run and don't look back," I tell her. "It'll be fine. Just find Mrs. Amber and have her call Dad."

She watches me for what seems like forever before she finally nods and answers me. "Okay."

"And remember to run." Fuck, I'm going to cry. I'm not going to get to see this beautiful, wild child grow into a woman. I'm not going to get to teach her all the things.

"I will," she promises, and this last bit is going to kill me, but I have to hold on, because I have to see her to safety.

"And I love you more than anything in this world," I say quietly, but I know she hears me.

"Mom," Rachel says again, sounding more than a little alarmed now, but there's no time to explain.

"Someone's coming," I whisper as I move her to stand in the corner. I grab one of the metal folding chairs and lift it over my head, ready to strike. "Just remember."

AIDE-DE-CAMP INJURED IN HUNTING ACCIDENT

CHAPTER 25

Thwarted plans

Everything seems to happen in slow motion, but I guess that's always how it plays out.

The doorknob slowly turns. Rachel is practically shaking where she's standing behind the door. My girl is trying so hard to be brave, and I'm so very proud of her. I would tell her so, but there's a ringing in my ears.

"Shh," I whisper, and she nods.

But the person who steps into the room shocks the absolute shit out of me. Although I guess I shouldn't be surprised. Rick told me to be careful around him.

"Come on," Captain Black says quietly. "We have to go now."

I watch him warily. Rick said not to trust him, but if we don't get out of this house, Rachel won't have a chance to run. I guess it all comes down to the devil you know and the devil you don't. And I know I don't want to be held in this house with the psychotic Ashley Jeffries any longer.

"What are you waiting for?" he snaps. "Come on."

"Okay," I say. "Come on, Rachel. We have to go now."

"Come on. We gotta move," he says in his slow southern drawl.

It's the gunshot that I didn't see coming.

One minute, I was setting down the chair and Rachel and I were going to have to trust Captain Black to get us out of here, and the next, Ashley is standing there with a smoking gun.

Black clutches his chest where the bullet must have left his body, because she shot him from behind. The look on his face is one of surprise. Me too. I did not see that shit coming, and I should have.

"Oh fuck!" she screams, and I have no idea what she has to scream at me about. I'm not the one who just shot a man.

Captain Black crumples forward, his face on the plain utilitarian gray carpet. His breathing is shaky. He doesn't look so good. But for now, he's alive.

"Look what you made me do!" She's panicking. Panic never helps in a situation like this. I should know; I watched a lot of *Hart to Hart* reruns late at night when I couldn't sleep because I was thinking about how much I missed Rick.

"This is okay," I say, trying to reassure a fucking murderer. How is this even my life right now? Oh fuck, now *I'm* panicking a little. "It'll be okay. Just let us go."

"No!" she hollers. "Fuck. You ruined everything. They're going to kill me now." I'm not going to feel bad for her, because she's involved with some pretty heavy stuff and is probably going to die. I'm pretty sure she just killed the president's aide-de-camp. That's not going to go over well. Not to mention, she is going to kill me and my daughter if I can't come up with another plan. Still, I'm not going to tell her any of this.

"Who's going to kill you?" I ask her, giving her my best impression of being sympathetic. Maybe if she feels like we're a team here, she will cave and let us go. "We can still fix this."

"It can't be fixed, you dumb cow!" she yells, waving the gun around while she screams. "I have to figure out what to do!" Ashley whirls out the door, slamming it behind her. I wait a second and test the handle, but it won't turn. Of course, in her wild mental state, she would manage to have the wherewithal to lock the goddamn door.

I'm pretty sure I don't want to know what her solution to this "problem" is going to be, because I think it ends with me in a body bag, and I'd really like to not help facilitate that. But the fact remains.

I have no other plan.

FUNERAL PLANS ARE PENDING

CHAPTER 26

Plans and the end

I need a plan.

My plans keep changing, and I don't like that. I'm great at adapting to my surroundings in order for survival, but this is excessive even for me. First, my plan was to get her out of the house and to Amber, but then Amber helped kidnap me, not that I blame her. Ashley put her in a tough spot.

My second plan was to attack Ashley when she came in the room so Rachel could run. I knew Ashley had a gun and would kill me, but it was a sacrifice I was willing to make in order to get Rachel to safety. But then Captain Black came in and tried to help us escape. I thought he was a bad guy, but he wasn't, which is too bad, because then Ashely shot him before losing her damn mind and locking us all in this little room again.

So now I need another plan. I don't have much time. Ashley looked to be a woman on the edge. And the fact that she kept ranting about how "they" were going to kill her leads me to believe she is not the mastermind here. Not that I ever thought she was. She's crazy, to be sure, but she's also dumb as shit. There's no way she could have come up with a plot to kidnap my child, let alone blackmail the president into passing some crazy bill that gives our enemies all our money and power and weapons.

"Mom, is he dead?" God, why does she have to ask all the tough questions today? I don't know how to tell her that a man who she's only even seen and not met just died in front of her trying to save us.

"Uhh…" I start, but he pushes up to roll over, surprising us both.

"Not quite," he groans and winces as he leans back against the small daybed. "Shi— ahh, shoot, that hurts."

"In these circumstances, Captain Black, you may say shit in front of my child," I tell him, making her giggle, so it was totally worth it.

"You can call me Ryan," he says in a strained Texas drawl.

"I'm sorry I thought you were a bad guy, Ryan."

"It's all right. So does your husband," he says, and his breath catches. It must hurt him to breathe. Contrary to his talking, I'm not sure he's doing so well. His face is ashen, and he looks to be out of breath. The fact of the matter is, he was shot and could die any second now.

"He does," I admit, and it makes me feel really guilty. Ryan just smirks.

"It's okay," he says shakily. "I wanted everyone to think I could be bad. It makes it easier to flush out the actual bad guy."

"Oh yeah, how's that working out for you?" I ask, folding my arms across my chest.

"Not so good." He laughs and then gasps. "It got me shot. I hate getting shot. It stings like a bitch."

"I said you could say 'shit' not 'bitch,'" I admonish him.

"My apologies for the words that come out of this old marine."

"Apology accepted."

"Thank you kindly," he says. "Now what are we going to do to get this little lady out of here?"

"I don't know," I admit.

"I think you had the right way of it earlier when you thought I was the crazy b—witch," he says, changing his word at the last minute. God, he's such a good guy. He tried to rescue us and got shot, and he's still trying to watch his language in front of my kid, even though he's clearly in agony.

"I was thinking that too," I tell him. I can feel the sad look on my face. "I guess it's just you and me."

"Oh don't look so sad," he says. "I'm glad to go out

with my boots on."

"Thank you."

"It's nothing," he says, brushing off my heavy words, and tips his head in the direction of Rachel, who is sitting at the table coloring like nothing is wrong. "But I think you should get ready, if you know what I mean. That crazy chick will be back soon."

Shit. I'm going to have to prepare her again, but this time I won't have the element of surprise on my hands. She's a smart kid, and she's going to understand right away that Mom isn't coming with.

"Hey, Rachel?" I ask as I walk around to squat in front of her again.

"Yes, Mom," she answers, but she doesn't look up at me.

"Remember what we were talking about earlier before Captain Black came in?"

"You were telling me to run when I get the chance and don't look back," she says. "Before trying to tell me that you weren't coming too."

"Yes, that's right, my darling girl."

"I don't like it," she says. "I want you to come with me."

"I want that too, honey." Oh, God, how much I want that, but it's just not possible. I don't know of another way.

"But you won't?" she asks softly.

"I can't, honey," I tell her honestly. "But if I could,

I would be with you always. You're my number one. Which is why I have to do this."

"Not come with me?" she asks hesitantly. I can see she's unsure in her beautiful eyes, and I have to give her the confidence to act bravely and be bold.

"Right, sweet girl," I answer. "When I tell you, you're going to run, just like we talked about. Don't look back, just run."

"Yes, Mommy," she says, and her little voice catches. I hate that she knows. Even though we haven't spoken the words, this perceptive child knows she won't see me again.

"Whatever you do, don't look back."

"Okay," she agrees softly.

"Find Daddy," I remind her. "He loves you so much, and he'll take care of you. Daddy will keep you safe."

"Okay, Mom. I will."

"Whatever you do, don't stop running," I say again. I hate the words, but I want to say them over and over so she knows what she needs to do. "No matter what you hear."

"I won't."

"That's my brave girl," I tell her as I pull her into my arms and hold her tight. "And know that I love you. No matter what."

"I love you too."

"I hear footsteps," I tell her, and fuck, I hate this,

but I'm ready to go. I'll do anything to save my child. Anything. Rick will raise her and care for her. I've seen the way he is with her, and he's as I always knew he would be—a wonderful father. I'm only sorry I won't be here to see it. "Get ready."

"I don't want to leave you, Mommy," Rachel says. She's starting to get upset, because she knows we won't see each other again after this.

"I'll be fine," I lie. "I have Captain Black—"

"Ryan," he corrects. "I think we're on a first-name basis now."

"I have Ryan," I correct my previous comment. "Just be ready."

"You did a good thing," Ryan whispers to me so Rachel can't hear him. I don't answer him; I just nod and get prepared for battle.

Rachel hides next to the hinges of the door, ready to sprint around it once I clobber Ashley with the folding chair. I test the weight of it in my hands. I'm as ready as I'll ever be. My knees are bent, and I can't hear anything but my heart pounding in my ears.

"I need the brat!" Ashley hollers, her voice sounding like it's just on the other side of the door. I don't know what she wants Rachel for, and I don't care. She's not getting her.

"It's going to be okay," I whisper to my baby. "Just remember what I said."

Rachel just nods.

The knob turns and the door swings open, and then everything happens all at once.

"Ashley, stop!" Rick shouts, and my blood freezes in my veins.

No! I want to scream. He isn't supposed to be here. I need him to be all right so he can take care of Rachel. She will need a parent to love her and look after her. As Ashlcy turns toward him, raising the gun in her hands, I swing the chair into her head and hear a crack.

"Now!" I shout at Rachel.

Our daughter runs in between where Ashley is lying on the floor and through the door. Rick pulls Rachel into him, holding her so she can't see the mess her mother made out of another human being.

"It's over," he says softly. "Don't look."

"I had to," I mumble as my whole body shakes. I had to kill her. It was her or me. I just wanted Rachel to escape. I never meant to kill anyone. I've never killed anyone before, and I never want to ever again.

I can't stop staring at the mess on the floor.

"Come here," Rick orders, still holding our daughter tight in his arms.

"I had to," I whisper.

And then everything goes black.

VEGAS WEDDING BELLS RING FOR MR. & MRS. DONOVAN.

Couple Exchanges Vows in Front of Powerful Friends.

EPILOGUE

"This is it," Grace says to me. "Are you ready?"

"Absolutely."

"I was hoping you'd say that," she says, handing me a huge bouquet of pink and white roses.

Yesterday, Rick, Rachel, and I flew to Las Vegas and checked into the biggest suite known to man in the Paris Hotel. It's actually two bedrooms larger than the apartment we shared when we were first married. After that, our friends started arriving.

Last night, we dressed in our best and had a fabulous dinner filled with steak and wine and good friendships. Rachel was over the moon getting to stay up late and party with her favorite pals, Jules and Grace.

But this morning was my absolute favorite.

We woke up and had an amazing breakfast, and then the hair and makeup ladies showed up. They looked a little terrified, probably because they had to go through a thousand pounds of security clearances to get this gig, but we made it worth their while. They can never tell the stories from today, because of the ironclad NDAs they signed, but they had so much fun with us that they didn't look like they cared.

Now, Grace and Jules are wearing beaded gowns in a muted shimmery gold. Rachel and I are in a rose gold. My dress is fitted and sleeveless with a deep V in the front and a deeper V in the back. Rachel's has cap sleeves and a poofy skirt. When we asked her what she wanted for our wedding, she said pink and sparkly. She should know by now not to give me a challenge like that. Her mama knows how to shop.

Grace gifted me with a pair of nude Louboutins—her signature shoe. I wore Rick's diamond studs and a black leather jacket I hand-painted on the back two skeletal hands intertwined and in gold script above them said *Til death do us part.*

Which brings us to now. I take my flowers and stand at the end of the line outside the little wedding chapel Rick and I were married in years ago. The music starts, and Jules walks through the door and down the aisle followed by Grace. We decided to shake things up a bit. Rachel and I are anything but go-with-the-flow girls. So instead of her walking ahead of me, we walk hand-in-hand toward the man who completes our family.

We didn't invite many people. The only seats filled are Wes and his beautiful wife Claire, Lee, who I hadn't met yet, Ryan—it was touch and go, but he made it out, although not without several expletives escaping while the paramedics loaded him into the ambulance—Gus, and Joe. Their roles as Jake's Secret Service agents were filled by other agents tonight so they could attend our wedding. And with special permission from the President of the United States, every man wore their dress blues. They aren't the whites Rick wore the first time, but I was also told it's the wrong season. I'll take what I can get.

As we walk down the aisle, Rick only has eyes for Rachel and me, and he smiles like I haven't seen him smile in years.

We repeat the same vows we did years ago, which is more symbolic than legal, seeing as how Rick also announced last night he never signed our divorce papers, which is why he carried my rings with him all of these years. Apparently, he got rip-roaring drunk then got really pissed and lit them on fire. I was on the run, so I never knew.

Then he slides my plain gold ring up my finger followed by my diamond band, which I'm more than happy to have back, but then he further surprises me by sliding the mother of all diamonds onto my finger as well.

"We have a past and a present, baby," he says quietly to me in front of our closest friends. "But most importantly, we have a future, and it is bright."

We may not have fully uncovered the plot against the president, but we're living in the moment. We're all doing our best to find our little bit of light in the darkness. And I have a feeling that everything will work out all right. Eventually. For now, Lee is looking more like he swallowed a lemon, and Ryan is eyeing Jules like she's a cool drink of water and he's a man who just walked out of a desert. It's still a little jarring since Rick and I were so convinced that he was a bad guy even when Jake swore up and down that Ryan was solid.

As it turned out, he saw the note I had left on the kitchen counter and realized that I was going off "half cocked" as he so delicately put it from his hospital bed. Apparently, Ryan realized that I didn't want Rick to get hurt and was sacrificing myself for the two people I love more than anything in this world. He also decided that that was bullshit, again, his words. Apparently, the big bad Marine developed a soft spot for my growly husband and figured that he needed to keep me safe for Rick's health. Rick swears it's some bullshit about Marines always needing to be the first in the fight. Usually the dispute dissolves into name calling around there.

But now, I can't help the smile that's spreading across my face and the big Texan glares in the direction of Jules, our very New York gal with brass balls and all. I can't help but feel like they're going to be so much fun to watch if they can ever stop fighting long enough to fuck.

Life is weird, but it'll all work out.

And when the minister tells Rick he can kiss his bride, boy does he ever. And then he scoops Rachel up onto his shoulders, where she lets out a battle cry that would make William Wallace proud, he takes my hand in his, and we head out into our future as a family. And he was right—it is bright, because it's ours. We never strayed, even when we were apart, because we were always it for each other and that will never change.

This is the forever we were always meant to have, and we're living it.

Thank you so much for reading ***Caught by the Chief of Staff***! I hope you loved Cara and Rick as much as I did. Jules and her mystery man are up next. You can read their story, ***The Press Secretary's Passion***. And if you haven't met Jake and Grace you're not too late. Pick up The Senator's Secret for more.

And last but never least, if you loved Wes you can read his story for FREE in ***Tell Me a Story***. I?ll see you all in June! Xo, Jen

PLAYLIST

Don't Start Now—Dua Lipa

One Beer—Lauren Alaina

Come Over—Sam Hunt

Fight—Taylor Parks and Florida Georgia Line

One Last Time—Ariana Grande

Marry You—Bruno Mars

Waking Up in Vegas—Katy Perry

Heartless—The Weeknd

Try—P!nk

Hot N Cold—Katy Perry

I Knew You Were Trouble—Taylor Swift

Never Really Over—Katy Perry

Strong Enough—Sheryl Crow

Heartless—Diplo featuring Morgan Wallen

Broken and Beautiful—Kelly Clarkson

Part of Me—Katy Perry

Marry Me—Martina McBride & Pat Monahan

The Bones—Maren Morris featuring Hozier

THE PRESS SECRETARY'S PASSION

"*Ohhh... Yes, Yes!*"

I watch as a strong masculine hand thrusts two fingers into my pussy. My hips arch up to meet him. Swirling whisps of color tease and twirl around his arm in the form of a tattoo but from this angle, you can't tell what it is in the video but I clearly have firsthand knowledge of the soldier's cross tattoo that sits on that tanned stretch of skin.

"*Please!*" I hear myself beg.

"*Mmm,*" he chuckles, low and throaty because he was enjoying teasing me, keeping me on the edge.

"*Please!*" I needed him so badly. Truth be told, I still do and thankfully, he's inclined to oblige me because he shows up in the middle of the night almost every night.

My cheeks heat and I try to clench my thighs without anyone noticing, *but he notices*. I see him smirk out of the corner of my eye. He knows what he does to me and how well he does it too. I watch the screen as he grips his thick, veiny cock in his fist before rubbing the flushed tip through my wetness and then up to stroke my clit making me bite my lip to keep from crying out because my torture only seems egg him on.

It's weird being both humiliated and turned on in a room full of your friends and colleagues but it's also nothing that I'm new to. I had a full career as a prime time anchor for Eagle News Network, a National Cable News Channel based out of New York before Jake named me his Press Secretary. You don't make it that far without a few scars on your arms and knives in your back. Although, even I have to admit that this one takes the cake.

My parents are going to kill me.

"*Ahhh,*" I moan as he finally notches the very tip of him at my center and slides in all the way. That sound is embarrassing. It's a high keening sound kind of like a cat in heat, although I guess that's not an inaccurate assessment.

"Kill me now," I mumble under my breath.

I remember the moment so well, not only because he showed me a repeat performance last night, but because it was that memorable. He had my body strung so tight and pushed me higher and higher. I was like a live wire on a bomb.

The muscles in his thighs and ass flex and ripple as he pulls out to the tip only to thrust back in making my tits bounce like a porn star. Is that what I am now? A porn star? He grips my hips so tight in his hands that

I wore marks for days just like the ones I carry on my skin now under my wool slacks.

I feel my eyes glaze over. I'm lost in the moment watching as he pumps into me over and over again. I watch as my hands grip the sheets of the hotel bed tight as I arch my back as he fucks me into oblivion.

And then I watch with everyone else as my jaw drops down on a silent scream and my eyes close as I find completion in a mystery man's arms.

Jake clears his throat. "I think we've seen enough," he says uncomfortably and the staffer holding the iPad in his hands hits pause.

"The video was released thirty-seven minutes ago," the staffer says helpfully. "And has been viewed twenty-six million times."

There's a knock at the door.

"Come in," Jake says.

"I was looking for Jules," my assistant says as he pokes his head in the room. "The Press Room is ready for you to brief them on HB 2250."

"Great," I say, not feeling it at all.

"You don't have to go in there, Jules," Jake says gently. "We can send in someone else. Hell, I'll do it myself."

"Normally, I would say no to that," Rick adds. "But for you, I'd even do it."

"Come on guys," I laugh but it lands flat even to my own ears. "This happens every day. I'll be old news by tomorrow. Time to get back on the horse."

"Jules, you don't have to be brave in here," Jake says. He knows me well for someone who's new to my life. Marrying my bestie, Grace, was the smartest thing he ever did and he loves her so much he'd do anything for her. Including protect her idiot best friend from a sex tape scandal.

I shrug my shoulder like it's no big deal. "Nah, I can't let them smell my fear. Besides, I'm surprised it hasn't happened before now."

And then I walk out of the Oval Office and down the hall towards the White House Press Room to brief a bunch of great white sharks on a Congressional Bill that the President vehemently opposes and plot twist, all while my boobs are bouncing around the internet like a porn star and the knowledge that the world has now seen my "O" face.

ALSO BY JENNIFER

A Presidential Affair
The Senator's Secret
Caught by the Chief of Staff
The Press Secretary's Passion

The Claire Goodnite Series
Tell Me a Story
Tuck Me in Tight
Say a Sweet Prayer
Kiss Me Goodnight
By the Light of the Moon
The Complete Claire Goodnite Series

The Liam Goodnite Series
Hush Little Baby
Don't Say a Word

The Funerals and Obituaries Series
I Met a Girl
Dead and Buried
Dead and Gone
Dead and Deceived
Dead and ... Wed?

The Murder on Ice Series
Attack Zone
Layback

The Southern Heartbeats
Stand, Volume 1
Joy
Whiskey Lullaby, Volume 2
Mercy
Just a Dream, Volume 3, Coming 2021

Stand Alone Titles
Trap: A Salvation Society Novel

ABOUT THE AUTHOR

Jennifer is a thirty-something lover of words, all words: the written, the spoken, the sung (even poorly), the sweet, the funny, and even the four-letter variety. She is a native of San Diego, California where she grew up reading the Brownings and *Rebecca* with her mother and *Clifford and the Dog who Glowed in the Dark* with her dad, much to her mother's dismay.

Jennifer is a graduate of California State University San Marcos, where she studied Criminology and Justice Studies. She is also a member of Alpha Xi Delta.

Thirteen years ago, she was swept off her feet by her very own sailor. Today, they are happily married, and the parents of an eleven-year-old and nine-year-old twins. She lives in East Texas, where she can often be found on the soccer or baseball fields, drawing with her children, reading, or wondering what the hell her favorite senior citizens have gotten up to now. Jennifer is convinced that if she puts her Fitbit on one of the dogs, she might finally make her step goals.

She loves a great romance, an alpha hero, and lots and lots of laughter.

STALK HER
(She loves that shit)

Website
www.jenniferrebeccaauthor.com

Facebook
www.facebook.com/JenniferRebeccaAuthor

Instagram
www.instagram.com/JenniferRebeccaAuthor

Twitter
www.twitter.com/JenniRLreads

Pinterest
www.pinterest.com/JenniferRebeccaAuthor

Bookbub
www.bookbub.com/authors/jennifer-rebecca

Book+Main
www. bookandmainbites.com/JenniferRebecca

And join her reader group on Facebook:
The Dangerous Dames
www. facebook.com/groups/JRdangerousdames

ACKNOWLEDGEMENTS

Thank you! Thank you so much for reading Caught by the Chief of Staff! I hope you loved Rick and Cara and their story as much as I did. Rick might be my very favorite hero ever and that's saying something. But don't count Jules' mystery hero out yet. He just might surprise you. Or not. ;)

I am so blessed to get to work with such an amazing team of people. Kayla, you walked into my life and became a dear friend. Thank you for keeping me on the straight and narrow even when modern colloquialisms kick my ass. "Cry me a table." Tricia, you are a lifesaver. You are smart, creative, and just a wonderful human being. Thank you for absolutely everything. And last but not least, the lady who wears so many hats (PR, marketing, Cover Design, Formatting, Business Partner, Bestie, Platonic Lifemate), Alyssa, this month has been weird. We haven't seen each other, but we've called more, we message more, and we're still family. I miss you seeing your face, I miss the meetings where magic happens, but I know that when this is all over, we'll celebrate because I couldn't do any of this without you by my side and I thank God every day that I don't have to. Now finish your book so I can throw you a damn party.

Thank you to my parents who helped me with my kids so that I could finish this book on time which is a miracle in itself let alone when there's a global pandemic to deal with. They are amazing and if we haven't killed each other after this quarantine business I'm going to owe them a fantastic dinner. I literally couldn't have done it without them and their help and love. And for keeping my small humans alive.

And because I always save the best for last like the icing on a cupcake, thank you to my amazing husband Sean for showing me every day what real love is, that fairy tales are real and that they exist in the every day, in the caring for each other. Thank you for encouraging me, for pushing me when I need it, and believing in me when I don't. I love you forever. It was only ever you.

www.ingramcontent.com/pod-product-compliance
Lightning Source LLC
Chambersburg PA
CBHW050857130726
47900CB00013B/187